Raider shivered.

It was chilly at this altitude, even though the calendar showed that fall should be several weeks
away. Raider flipped back the hem of the heavy
woolen blanket that lay over the bunk, and crawled
beneath the cover.

He stiffened and his breath hissed through his teeth
in surprise.

From the darkness very close to his ear he could
hear a low chuckle.

It was already warm under the blanket. The warmth
was that of flesh.

And now that he thought about it, he could identify
his visitor by the light fragrance he remembered
from lunch. The scent had been in his nostrils all
afternoon in memory. Now it was here beside him.

He reached out a hand and encountered bare, warm,
exceptionally soft skin...

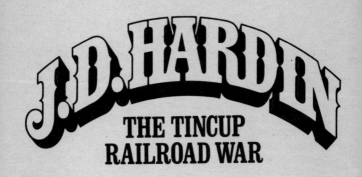

J. D. HARDIN

THE TINCUP
RAILROAD WAR

BERKLEY BOOKS, NEW YORK

THE TINCUP RAILROAD WAR

A Berkley Book/published by arrangement with
the author

PRINTING HISTORY
Berkley edition/December 1985

ISBN: 0-425-08669-0

PRINTED IN THE UNITED STATES OF AMERICA

CHAPTER ONE

"I don't like this," Raider said. He slouched lower into the soot-smeared upholstery of his seat and frowned as he watched yet another burning coal ember flutter through the open window of the passenger car. The ember landed on the seat cushion beside his right thigh and lay there glowing, burning a small, black hole into the dirty maroon fabric. His humor was such that he watched it burn itself out rather than extinguish it with a fingertip or brush it aside. The problem and the responsibility for such things, after all, belonged to the Denver, South Park, and Pacific.

Doc Weatherbee, beside him, suppressed a twisted smile. Doc was fully aware of his tall companion's reasons for displeasure, but he pretended to misunderstand. "How could you not like it?" he asked, craning his neck to see past Raider in the window seat. "Gorgeous scenery, perfectly adequate accommodation, a passing fair lunch even if the trout were a trifle overcooked." He shook his head in feigned wonder. "I fail to see, old man, how you could not be comfortable."

Raider scowled at him, keeping his eyes directed inside the railway car and refusing to look outside. If he had looked out at the country they were passing through, he might have had to admit that it was as beautiful as Doc claimed. And he wanted to make no such damned admissions. Not right now. They were descending from South Park toward Buena Vista, high in the Rocky mountains. Outside Raider's window were the Buffalo Peaks. Below them lay the Arkansas River valley. And beyond it, peak after white-capped peak of a towering mountain range where most of the tips had been named for eastern universities like Harvard and Princeton. That small fact irritated Raider too at the moment, if only because it probably pleased Weatherbee.

"You know damn good an' well what I don't like about this an' why I don't like it," Raider snapped.

"Nonsense," Doc lied happily.

"Bastard," Raider mumbled. He lapsed into a sullen silence while the narrow gauge train slid smoothly down the tracks toward the end of the line.

Doc hid a smirk and, knowing it would rub salt into the wounds of Raider's ill humor, pulled a cigar from his pocket. Raider grunted something that Doc was probably well off not hearing. The tall operative turned sideways in his seat, presenting his back to Weatherbee and closing his eyes in a halfhearted gesture of rest rather than look out the damned window.

Doc grinned for a moment. Then his expression became more serious as he thought about Raider's complaints.

Actually, Weatherbee reflected, this time his foul-tempered partner almost had reason for his humor.

Doc did not like the assignment a whole hell of a lot either.

He sighed and amended that thought.

It was not the *assignment* to which he objected, although Raider, being Raider, would probably find something wrong with that, too.

To Doc Weatherbee's way of thinking, it was the gold-plated anus they were performing the assignment *for* who drew a certain amount of distaste.

But Wagner had been quite specific about the case when both of them had tried to beg off it. *No* Pinkerton operative really wanted to work for Rutherford Welles. And Welles had demanded Weatherbee and Raider by name.

Doc sighed again. This assignment appeared to be their "reward" for having successfully concluded a case on Welles' behalf some time ago.

That had been when Welles was a vice-president for a large and well-established railroad line. Now the man was having visions of grandeur. Or something. Now, according to Wagner, Mr. T. Rutherford Welles was building his very own railroad empire. Or trying to.

There were problems with the proposed new line, obviously, and now he had come running to the Pinkerton Agency, to Doc and Raider, for the help he needed to put his narrow gauge empire across the peaks and into mining country not yet reached by the Denver, South Park, and Pacific or the still larger Denver and Rio Grande, both of which had already driven steel as far as Buena Vista on the banks of the Arkansas.

Precisely what kind of trouble Welles was having with his line, Doc did not know. Nor had Wagner. Welles' telegraphed messages had been more frantic and demanding than they had been informative.

Frantic and demanding, Doc thought. That was almost a description of Rutherford Welles himself. When they had worked with the man before they had found him to be passionate in his pursuit of very nearly anything that came to his attention. Passionate to the point of being frantic about it, regardless of whether he was in the right or in the wrong. And certainly demanding. He wanted his results, and he wanted them *now*.

Welles had demanded a particular team of operatives for

this assignment and therefore was likely paying extra for the privilege of having them at his command—at least he was if Doc knew anything at all about Allan Pinkerton— and Doc shuddered to think what effect that might have on Rutherford Welles and his level of patience.

No, Doc thought, just this once Raider might almost be right to be unhappy with an assignment.

Doc used a gold-plated nipper—a present from a female admirer of recent and vigorous acquaintance—to remove the twisted tip from his cigar, then struck a match to light it. He exhaled with satisfaction and was rewarded with a grunt of displeasure from the seat beside him. Raider hunched his shoulders lower and said something under his breath, but he did not deign to look at his seatmate and partner at his side.

That response, Doc thought happily, was one of the more sane reasons for smoking. He settled lower in his seat and put his left foot into the aisle, pausing for a moment to admire the gleam of polish on his shoe tip before he crossed his right ankle over his left, careful as he did so to avoid mussing the crease in his trousers. Doc Weatherbee was as content as he could reasonably expect to be.

They collected their things from the baggage car, and this time it was Raider's turn to put the needle to Doc.

"Onliest damn thing that I approve o' this whole stinking mess," Raider gloated.

"And what would that be?" Doc asked, falling into Raider's trap.

"That damn mule an' your hoorah wagon. Denver's the place they both belong, by damn. With any luck somebody will've had sense enough to bust that fool wagon up for firewood 'fore we get back, an' the damn mule will turn out where she belongs too. In a bar o' soap."

Doc choked back the reply he wanted to utter. He was inordinately fond of his mule Judith. And Raider knew it.

Instead he snatched up his Gladstone bag and turned his back on Raider, setting off at a fast walk toward the hotel.

Doc had objected strenuously to Wagner's demands that he leave Judith and his wagon behind.

"The terrain is not likely to be suitable," Wagner had said, "and we have no intention of paying outrageous boarding fees up there plus the outlay for horse rental." He had been insistent about it, and in the end Doc had had to leave Judith behind along with all the equipment he customarily carried in his wagon.

With Pinkertons, Doc had long since learned, the end of any argument—the beginning too, for that matter—was apt to come from the ink on an accounting ledger. This even though the client was responsible for the reimbursement of expenses. Allan Pinkerton was as close with a client's purse as with his own. Which, Doc acknowledged, might well have been a minor contributing factor in the agency's popularity.

Doc marched up to the desk of the Harrington House and registered as a guest. His reservation had been made in advance by wire.

Raider had not been half a dozen paces behind him and quickly joined him at the desk.

"I have your room ready for you, Mr. Weatherbee," the clerk said. "A single?" He eyed Raider, who was standing expectantly at Doc's side.

"That is correct," Doc said. He ignored Raider.

"Very good, sir." The clerk handed Doc a key. "Room 29, sir. Second floor front."

Doc picked up his Gladstone and moved toward the stairs. Behind him he could hear a conversation developing. Something about reservations . . . lack of rooms . . . so sorry.

Raider bellowed.

Doc smiled.

Weatherbee continued up the stairs toward his room. His *single* room.

Doc had tried to tell the thick-headed, thin-skinned Raider about the usefulness of advance notice, but the man had not wanted to take the time away from his sordid diversions. Which was entirely his affair, of course. Doc smirked a little at the thought of his own pun.

And of course Raider was a big boy now, quite capable of fending for himself. So let him.

Doc let himself into the spacious, well-appointed hotel room and was pleased with what he found there. He was already looking forward to dinner at the Harrington House. Roast duck, perhaps, with an oyster dressing. Or veal. They had a way with veal here. He smiled again.

CHAPTER TWO

Raider shouldered his way into the Harrington House restaurant, brushing past a little man with a bundle of menus in his hand and ignoring the pipsqueak. Raider was in no mood for pleasantries this morning.

There the son of a bitch was. Sitting in a far corner of the place with rations enough for a troop of cavalry spread out in front of him. Sitting there dressed to the nines like he was fixing to go out for a Sunday stroll with the gentry. Raider set his jaw and stalked across the room toward Weatherbee.

His humor was not at all improved when he noticed another newcomer to the restaurant being seated at a table several yards from Weatherbee's.

She was young and pretty and was accompanied by an older woman who might have been an aunt. The dang girl's eyelids fluttered when she saw Weatherbee, and there was a quickly hidden hint of a smile on her dimpled cheeks before she ducked her head and gave her attention to the menu a waiter handed her. Raider saw the answering tug of smile at the corners of Doc's damned mouth, but the two did not speak. It was enough to make Raider suspicious. Suspicious? Hell, it was enough to make him furious.

Here Weatherbee had gone and spent the night surrounded by luxury—and who knew what else?—and his partner, to whom that ingrate Weatherbee owed so much, had had to bed down in a railside flophouse surrounded by a bunch of snoring drunks.

Son of a *bitch!* Raider thought as he helped himself to a seat at Doc's table without waiting for an invitation.

"Good morning," Weatherbee said cheerfully. "Have a biscuit? The strawberry jam is excellent." He shoved a small plate of biscuits toward Raider and then a cut glass bowl of jam with the handle of a tiny silver spoon protruding from it. Raider briefly considered upending the bowl on top of Weatherbee's groomed and brushed scalp.

Doc grinned at him. "Why don't you join me for breakfast. My treat, Rade."

Raider made a face and looked like he was about to spit.

Doc laughed. The fancy-pants peckerwood calmly returned to his meal.

Raider was about to say something but was interrupted by the appearance of a waiter at his elbow. As far as he could tell there seemed to be two waiters on duty in the damn place for every customer. It was annoying.

The waiter put a menu under his nose. Raider shoved it away. "Flannel cakes," he said. "A stack of 'em." He paused for a moment, wanting all of a sudden to stump these prissy so-and-sos. "An' some pork jowl fried just till the fat starts to curl. And coffee, barefoot."

"Of course, sir," the waiter said as if the order was the most perfect request possible. He smiled and went away.

"You passed a pleasant evening, I hope," Doc said.

Raider grunted something at him.

Doc smiled. "Ready to beard the lion?"

"I won't *never* be ready to go see that SOB Welles, if that's what you mean."

Doc sighed. From his expression it was plain that he was not looking forward to the morning's interview either. "Duty," he said lamely.

Raider grunted again.

When Raider's breakfast order came, the flannel cakes were slightly sweet and so light it took a dollop of jam to hold them down on the plate, and the dang jowls—*where* had they come up with *those* without warning, Raider had to wonder—were cooked to perfection. The coffee was steaming and aromatic and was served with refills ready in a small silver pot that matched the rest of the trash on the table. The elegance and the quality of the meal only served to deepen Raider's sour frame of mind as he thought once again about the differences between the night he had just spent and the one Weatherbee must have passed. But Raider would be damned to hell before he would ask Doc one *word* about the hotel or about that filly sitting several paces behind Raider's back. Be damned if he would.

Later Raider got a little satisfaction back out of the morning. He slipped the livery stable hostler half a buck to make sure Weatherbee was given an exceptionally fine-looking mount. Raider smiled a little. And one that had the disposition of a rattlesnake and a mouth that might have been lined with boilerplate steel.

They followed the directions they had gotten from the Denver and Rio Grande people in Buena Vista and rode south until they found the start of the Arkansas Valley, Tincup, and Pacific tracks, then turned west toward the massive, jutting wall of white-peaked mountains that rose before them.

"Impressive," Doc observed when they reached the beginning of the AVT&P tracks.

"Ain't it just," Raider agreed.

There was a shack built on the west side of the D&RG tracks but as yet no depot there. One section of siding had been laid, but there was no roundtable to turn the engines of the young railroad. There were some heavy timbers scattered on the ground where a roundhouse might someday be built, and there was a pile of raw lumber where a depot might someday be.

There were no workers in view at the site, however, and no activity was taking place at the moment.

"It ain't Sunday morning, is it?" Raider asked.

"Not unless we overslept rather severely," Doc said.

"Don't start with me about that again," Raider warned. His remark drew a smile but no comment from Doc. They rode a few paces on.

"Have you noticed," Doc asked, "that the Denver and Rio Grande has not seen fit to build a siding for freight transfer?"

"Uh huh. Kinda makes you think they want to wait a while and see does Mr. Welles have something to transfer before they go to the bother, don't it."

They rode on a little farther, Doc's hard-mouthed horse following at the side of Raider's mount.

"Notice something else back there?" Raider asked.

"What?"

"The lumber stacked where I reckon they'll want to put their station."

Weatherbee nodded. "Not dried too well, was it. The boards are already starting to warp."

Raider peered down toward the ground on his left, toward the set of rails they were following. "Ties look all right, though," he said.

"They don't seem to be warping," Doc agreed.

"And the steel, it looks to run straight."

Doc smiled. "What more could the man need then?"

"Can't think of a hell of a lot," Raider said. He bumped

his horse, a short-coupled red roan, into a jog. Doc's tall, straight-shouldered bay picked up the pace to stay with him, and Weatherbee began to bounce awkwardly at the choppy gait.

"Slow down, damn it," Doc hollered. "Or speed up. Something."

"Naw," Raider said happily. "This is just nice." He looked over his shoulder. Doc was right there, his bay keeping pace with the much better roan despite Weatherbee's hands, both of them, sawing at the reins trying to get the creature under some measure of control.

"Don't worry," Raider said. "We'll get there directly. Not more than an hour or so if those boys back at Buenie were right."

Weatherbee tried to say something that undoubtedly would have been unpleasant, but the words were chopped off in his throat. The two horses were traveling close enough together that Raider could clearly hear the clack of Doc's teeth jamming together as the stiff-legged bay stumbled and rattled Doc's brains.

Raider turned his head so Weatherbee could not see the smirk that pulled at the corners of his lips. The good roan wanted to stretch out into a lope, but Raider held him down to the trot, with Doc's tall bay following obediently in the same jarring pace.

Kind of made up for last night, Raider decided. Kind of did.

CHAPTER THREE

They could see T. Rutherford Welles' "field headquarters" well before they got there. A short siding had been built on the north side of the tracks, near a small creek and a thick grove of aspen trees. There were two cars parked on the siding. A thin curl of pale smoke came from a stovepipe at the end of one of the cars. There was no sign of an engine.

Raider let out a low whistle as they approached the nearer of the two cars, which they could now see were separated by a dozen feet of bare track rather than being linked together.

"Fan-damn-cy," Raider said.

"Rather," Doc said drily.

The nearer car gleamed with shiny maroon lacquer and bright, carved gilt-work. Velveteen drapes covered the windows, and an Oriental houseboy complete with waist-long pigtail appeared on the rear platform at the sound of their approach. The houseboy wore a white linen jacket and baggy black trousers. He was barefoot.

12

"Some setup, huh?" Raider said.

"Mr. Welles has a sound set of fiscal priorities," Doc said. "Cheap lumber for the depot but no scrimping on the boss's quarters, thank you."

Raider reined his roan to a halt, and Doc's bay stopped too. He glanced at Weatherbee in time to catch a look of distinct relief as Doc dismounted.

There was no hitch rail provided at the site of the private car, and only a complete fool will trust a rented horse to ground rein. They tied the animals to the rail surrounding the platform of the private car.

"Welcome, gentlemen," the houseboy said.

Raider's head snapped around at the light, almost lilting sound of the houseboy's voice. He took another look. And then a third.

The houseboy was a girl. The loose jacket and baggy britches did a fine job of concealing whatever figure the girl might have had, but now that he was looking closely he could see what might—or might not—have been small hidden bumps beneath the white linen of the jacket.

She was tiny. Probably would have had to wear shoes with built-up heels to make five feet. And her age could have been anything from fifteen to thirty-five for all Raider could tell.

But her voice and, on closer inspection, the unblemished satin of her skin showed that she was, indeed, a female house*boy*.

He could not see her face very well. She had her eyes cast down shyly. But he could see the curl of long, long lashes dark against the softness of her cheek. He got the impression that she would be quite pretty with her hair done less severely and in decent clothing. Or perhaps in none.

Beside him, Weatherbee said something that sounded like a cross between a cough and a hiccup. The girl's chin lifted suddenly, her eyes bright with pleased excitement, and she launched into a singsong burst of chatter.

"Sorry," Doc interrupted. "I apologize for not being able to speak your ancient and honored language. The phrase was merely something I picked up in San Francisco."

The girl stopped her chatter and again lowered her eyes, but she still looked pleased. "You have done me the kindness of bringing me joy, sir. Please accept my thanks." Her English was excellent, Raider noticed, with practically no trace of accent. "May I help the gentlemen?" she asked.

"We are from the Pinkerton Agency," Doc said. "We're here to see Mr. Welles. At his request," he added.

"Of course, sirs. Follow me, please."

Raider gave Doc a dirty look. After all, *he* had seen the girl first. Even if he had thought she was a boy at the time.

Weatherbee ignored him. By that time Doc was already on the platform and following the housegirl inside. Rade had to hurry to catch up.

The interior of the private car was as plush as the outside had hinted. Everything and anything that it was possible to carve and polish had been carved and polished. Everything else had been upholstered. The dominant colors—hell, the overwhelming colors—were scarlet and gold. It looked like a long, narrow New Orleans whorehouse. A fancy one. Raider decided he liked it. There were a lot of things worse than a New Orleans whorehouse.

The girl had them wait in a tiny vestibule built at the rear of the car. "One moment, please."

They could see past her perfectly well into the main salon of the private car. The salon occupied the full width of the car and took up probably half of its length. Raider thought he could probably imagine what kind of rooms would be in the front half of the car.

T. Rutherford Welles was ensconced in a deep, over-stuffed armchair at the far end of the salon. The man had a small table at one hand, the table holding a decanter of some liquor and a pair of glasses and a small tray of fruits and cheeses. On his other side was a woman.

Raider had to swallow hard to keep from staring. Then he decided what the hell. It was only normal and natural for him to stare.

She was . . . beautiful. Tall, full-bosomed, with high, swirling curls of raven-dark hair crowning her lovely head. She wore a gown, of a scarlet hue that very nearly matched the color of the flocked paper on the walls of the rail car, that showed an impossibly tiny waist and a swell of full breasts that were trying to spill out over the confinement of the cloth that more or less covered them. The gown was cut damn near low enough to check the color of her nipples.

She was—Raider swallowed—she was something. A cream-colored cameo was suspended in the pale valley between her breasts, and she had on long dangly earrings to match.

Raider wondered what color her eyes were. She was too far away for him to see. Unfortunately. He had time to get a good look at her while the little housegirl daintily approached T. Rutherford Welles and announced his guests. Although the slob could see them standing there perfectly well from where he sat, he refused to acknowledge them until they had been properly announced.

Raider took his eyes off the woman long enough to take a quick look at Welles.

The man had not changed a great deal since they had last seen him.

No, Raider amended, Welles had put on some more weight since then. The man's face was still flushed and full, reddened by wine and roasts of beef with thick gravy instead of by anything relating remotely to work or effort.

He had a walrus mustache and thick muttonchop sidewhiskers, and his hands glinted with the cold fire of diamonds reflecting light every time he moved a finger.

Welles knew how to dress. Raider had to give him that much. Likely it took half a herd of tailors in their prime to keep him suited out like he always was.

For sure, a man as big as he was could not, never mind would not, buy anything off a rack that would come close to fitting.

Because as big as he was in the gut, T. Rutherford Welles was even bigger for sheer height.

He was half a head taller than Raider, who was no small man himself. Raider looked at him again and decided that by now the SOB probably tipped the scales—livestock scales, since no human variety would be likely to hold him—at 350 or more.

T. Rutherford Welles was a man who liked to live well.

The diminutive housegirl announced the arrival of the Pinkertons, and Welles finally condescended to look at them. "Weatherbee. Raider," he roared. "Where the hell have you been?"

It was, Raider knew, as close as they could expect to receiving a cordial greeting from Mr. Welles.

Raider shouldered his way past Doc, who was still waiting to be invited into the sanctum of the salon, and stalked the length of the plush room. His glance flicked from the woman to Welles and back again. "We can leave if you want us to. Matter o' fact, Welles, I'll send the wire myself. Tell the office to send you a couple operatives you like better."

"Don't be foolish, my boy. I asked for you, didn't I? You're the ones to handle this." He turned to the woman. The housegirl had already disappeared toward the front of the car.

"Wanda," Welles said. "Make the gentlemen comfortable. Drinks. Whatever they want. And tell cook they'll be staying for lunch."

Wanda sat where she was for a moment gazing up with frank appraisal at the tall, lean Pinkerton man who loomed over her.

She saw a broad-shouldered, narrow-hipped man with

hair as black as her own. His eyes and mustache were strikingly dark against the deep tan of his weathered face. He wore jeans stuffed into tall boots and a scuffed leather jacket. His wide-brimmed Stetson was as black as his hair.

He was more ruggedly commanding than handsome, but he carried himself with a natural grace that belied the size of his six-foot-two frame. His movements were those of a predator, an impression that was emphasized by the dark, ready bulk of the .44-.40 revolver at his hip.

Wanda had a look of speculation in her eyes—they were green, Raider could see now—as she inspected him.

She looked him over from hat crown to boot heels and then let her eyes slide past him to Weatherbee, who had finally entered the salon to stand beside him.

Weatherbee was not quite as tall as his companion and was lighter of build, the cutting quickness of a blacksnake whip next to the strength and power of a hawser. His hair was pale, his eyes blue.

In contrast to his partner, Weatherbee was dressed nearly as well as T. Rutherford Welles in a dark gray worsted suit with tie and matching vest, pearl gray derby hat, and pale gray spats over highly polished shoes that he had managed to keep free of dust while they rode.

Doc was genuinely handsome where his partner was ruggedly masculine. He might well have been mistaken for a dandy by anyone who did not see the flashing, intense look that lay deep in his eyes.

Wanda rose. She smiled at Doc. But it was to Raider that she extended a gloved hand.

"Welcome, gentlemen." Her voice was throaty and sensuous. It had a curious timbre that made Raider think of locked doors and drawn curtains. "Would you care for something to drink?"

"Whiskey," Raider said, hoping it had not come out sounding like the croak of a frog. Wanda was standing so near in front of him that the tips of her breasts were brushing teasingly against his chest. Lordy, but she was a tall one. Her eyes were barely lower than his own. He looked into the clear green of them and thought that, if he dived inside, it would take him the better part of an hour to swim to the other side. But he also got the impression that such a trip would be worth the while.

"A decent claret would be nice," Doc said.

Wanda smiled. The effect of it was enough to make Raider's breathing come faster and heavier. "As you wish, gentlemen." She turned and drifted away in a swirl of skirts. Raider blinked and had some difficulty returning his attention to T. Rutherford Welles and the problems of the moment.

Welles tilted his head back and roared with laughter. Raider blinked again and managed to focus on the big man.

Welles chuckled. "Not bad for a country boy from Sacramento, eh, Raider? I thought you'd like that. But keep your hands off. Private stock, eh?" He winked lewdly and laughed again.

"Now," Welles said, "what do you boys have to report to me about the sons of bitches that've been holding up my rails?"

CHAPTER FOUR

There was a brief period of confusion. Welles was under the impression that Raider and Doc had already had time enough to work on his case and was convinced that by now they should have gotten it under control and been ready to drop off his payroll. Raider and Doc, in turn, were perplexed by his talk about holdups. Their scanty briefing had included nothing about train robberies.

Eventually, over a lunch of roast squab, they got things clarified.

"No, damn it, not 'holdups,'" Welles said around a mouthful of breast meat. "Delays. That's what I mean. Those sons of bitches are holding up my track construction. Deliberately. Of course I know who's doing it. That's as plain as plain can be. It's that bastard Finch."

Doc looked at Raider and raised an eyebrow. Raider shook his head. Neither of them had heard anything about anyone named Finch.

"All I want you boys to do—an' damn quick at the prices that damned Pinkerton charges—is put a stop to it. Just go up there and put a stop to it, that's all."

Doc accepted the offer of a roll from Wanda, who seemed to be acting as hostess at the table that had been brought into the salon by a pair of Chinese men and then laid by the housegirl. "Tell us more about this Finch," he requested while Wanda passed him the butter.

"It's all in the report I mailed to Pinkerton," Welles said with a wave of his hand. "All of it."

Doc refrained from showing the annoyance he felt. Welles was the same delightful fellow Doc remembered from the past. Arrogant and impatient and wholly uninterested in details—details like the amount of time it took for a packet to pass through the mails from Buena Vista, Colorado, to Chicago, Illinois, and back again to Denver. As far as Welles's type was concerned, once it left his hand the information in that packet should be known to all concerned.

Doc explained, patiently, the fact that they had seen no such information and the probable reasons for that.

"Shit," Welles said. Wanda, at the other end of the table, pretended not to have heard. "At these prices, by God, man has the right to expect some efficiency," Welles complained.

Doc restated Raider's earlier offer. "We can withdraw from the case if you prefer," he said. "Although I suspect your specific request for our assignment to the case is the reason it took so long to get someone onto it. I am sure there were other operatives nearer to hand when your request was made. We could still bring some of them in."

"No, damn it," Welles said. "I wanted you on it. Still do." He wiped a rim of grease from his lips with the back of his hand, and Doc winced. The man had a napkin in his lap; he could have used that.

Welles winked at him. "I know from before that you boys aren't squeamish about pulling a trigger. And you don't always follow the, uh, rules. If you know what I mean."

"As a matter of fact, sir, I do *not* know what you mean," Doc said with dignity. Although the truth was that he probably did. If he remembered correctly, and he was sure he did, the last time they had been involved with T. Rutherford Welles there had been a bit of rough business at hand. And Raider, darn him, had leaped into it tooth and nail. Doc was very much afraid that Mr. Welles had gotten a mistaken impression of the Pinkerton Agency's operations.

Welles grunted and winked again. "Whatever you say, Weatherbee. Just so you know what's going on here and get out there and handle it."

"But we do not know what your problem is, Mr. Welles. Not entirely." He shifted his glance toward Raider, who was paying attention not to the head of the table but to the other end, where Wanda was engaged in the dissection of a thigh. Doc hoped, forlornly, that Raider was not going to be stupid enough to take a crack at Welles' "private stock."

"I already told you," Welles said. "It's that damned Finch."

"We still do not know who Finch is."

Welles dismissed Doc's ignorance with a wave of a tiny drumstick. "Finch, damn it. Corey Finch. Runs a half-assed little freight outfit up in the mining camps. As quick as my rails reach Tincup, Finch is out of business. He knows it; I know it; anybody with half a brain knows it. Soon as my line is in, Finch is out. He can't hope to compete with my prices for haulage. Not with wagons and mules, he can't. And of course the payrolls. It takes a hell of a lot of men to haul by wagon. I can undercut him until he bleeds and still recoup my investment in a year or less at the rate they're wanting to drag ore down out of those mountains. You understand that, don't you? There's a couple little shirttail stamp mills up there now that can't handle the load they already have and that only reduce the ore, don't really refine it. But once my railroad gets in, I can haul raw ore down to the smelters at Leadville for less than the price of taking it to the stamp mills the way things are now. And the mine operators will be recovering half again as much gold out of their ore as they can from a simple stamp mill. Which means my freight rates for ore haulage can be set at just damn near anything I want." Welles smiled and wiped his mouth again.

"That much I do understand," Doc said.

"I should hope so. So now the only problem is this Finch. You take care of him, I write Pinkerton a check, and there's no more problems."

"Just what is the problem, Mr. Welles?"

"I told you that already. Finch is holding up the construction of my rails, man. My crews get roadbed prepared, and some son of a bitch comes along behind them and blows the ledges or uses powder charges to drop higher ledges down onto my bed. My tie-cutting crews go up on the stinking hills to cut timber and somebody runs them off. Or shoots 'em. I've had, I don't know, half a dozen of my Chink boys killed up there. It slows the rest of them down, let me tell you."

Doc kept his face straight. "I am sure that it would," he said mildly.

He remembered now what it was that had brought Welles to power, not only on this line of his own but with the several other railroads he had worked with before.

After the Central Pacific was completed and linked to the Union Pacific years earlier, there had been a flood of suddenly out-of-work Chinese laborers glutting the labor markets of California. T. Rutherford Welles had somehow— probably with the help of a tong—contracted for the services of a number of those laborers. The man had taken his workers east and hired them out to other railroads under construction, first one and then another.

Their labor had been performed at half the cost of hiring Irish or German immigrants, and it had quickly become understood. Anyone who wanted to build a railroad and do it at the least possible expense should first hire T. Rutherford Welles and put him in charge of the work gangs.

Just how much of that labor capital Welles had been able to rake off for his own bank accounts was apparent now. Because building even a minor narrow gauge line like this one would be an enormously expensive undertaking. If Welles was really building the AVT&P with his own capital, he had been able to construct himself a nicely feathered nest indeed during those years.

"Do you have any proof that this, uh, Finch is the person responsible for your troubles, Mr. Welles?"

"Hell, yes," Welles said. "Common sense, man. That's my proof. Quick as I'm in, Finch is out. He hates my guts. He's said so in public plenty of times. He denies having anything to do with the sabotage, of course, but shit, you'd only expect that."

Doc automatically glanced down the table toward Wanda. It offended him for anyone to curse in the presence of a lady. Although, granted, it was probably stretching things a great deal to refer to Wanda as a lady. Still . . .

This time, however, the lady in question very likely had not heard the vulgarity uttered by her employer. She and Raider were leaning close together, whispering something. Wanda was laughing, and Raider looked entirely too pleased with himself.

Doc rolled his eyes heavenward. This kind of complication they did not need.

"Just you boys go up there and get Finch out of my hair," Welles was saying. "An' I don't much care how you do it, if you get my meaning." He winked again. "Matter o' fact, Weatherbee, there could be a little bonus in this if you and Raider act on it real quick. The kind o' bonus the Pinkerton Agency doesn't have to know about. If you know what I mean." The gross son of a bitch laughed, and Doc suppressed a shudder.

Welles' meaning was much too clear.

Doc was afraid, though, that the man was going to be in for a disappointment. Much as he might be able to say against his frequent partner—and the list was virtually end-less—Raider was no more of a hired assassin than was Doc Weatherbee. If that was what Welles expected, the man was simply out of luck.

"We have been hired to undertake an investigation in your behalf, Mr. Welles," Doc said calmly. "We shall do that. Our reports will reach you periodically through the Pinkerton Agency, and all remuneration should be channeled to us through them, sir."

Welles looked at him. Then tilted his head back and laughed. "If I didn't know better, Weatherbee, I'd begin to think you were a kind o' stuffy little bastard. But I do know better, don't I?" Welles laughed again and gave Doc another broad, conspiratorial wink.

Jesus, Doc thought. How could anyone convince this overstuffed toad that not everyone was like him?

For that matter, if anyone discovered the method for that enormous undertaking, would it be worth the trouble?

Probably not, Doc concluded. He took a final sip of his wine, which was acceptable but considerably short of ex-cellent, and nudged Raider. "We should be leaving now, Rade."

"Not so fast," Welles said.

"Is something wrong?"

"Only if you don't want to be shot by my boys," Welles said. "I've already wired up-track for my foreman to come get a look at you boys. Some o' my crews are getting touchy about strangers, 'specially strangers carrying guns, and I want you to get a proper introduction before you go messing about in my camps."

"This foreman fella's gonna escort us?" Raider asked, contributing to the luncheon conversation for the first time.

"Right," Welles said. "I wired for him to bring the engine back quick as the flatcars are unloaded. He'll be here this evening, and you can ride up-track with him in the morn-ing."

Raider seemed quite pleased by the idea of an overnight delay. Doc refused to speculate on the reasons for his partner's reaction, although he himself was less than happy with the plan. It seemed to him like an opportunity for Raider to get into trouble. Unless Doc could find some way to keep him out of it.

How to do that was the next question to be answered, Doc thought.

CHAPTER FIVE

Raider suffered through the afternoon and evening impatiently. The surroundings were all right, and the whiskey was okay, but his interests really were elsewhere.

He kept thinking about the soft, billowing, creamy orbs that had been trying to break free from the bodice of Wanda's dress at lunch.

Thinking about them but not seeing them.

Welles had taken the woman into the forward part of the private car immediately after lunch for some private "discussion." Raider had somewhat enviously thought he knew what kind of "discussion" would be taking place there. But unless Rutherford Welles was faster than a damn buck rabbit there had been no such goings-on. The man had taken Wanda to the front of the car and then reappeared, alone, in the salon a few minutes afterward. Raider had not seen Wanda since that time.

Now, with dinner behind them and the foreman on hand,

they were once again in the salon. The Chinese housegirl was handling the chores of serving drinks. There was still no sign of the delectable Wanda.

The foreman's name was Kent. Raider was not quite clear on whether that was his first name or his last, not that it made any difference. Raider did not particularly like him. They had absolutely nothing in common. The foreman seemed totally dedicated to one interest alone, and that was the laying of rails. Raider was not high on endless conversations about the laying of rails.

Even what little Kent was able to tell them about the recent sabotage attempts—attempts, hell: someone had been getting the job done pretty well in that area—he always had to relate to time lost and rails unlaid.

Let Weatherbee worry about ferreting out the details of the sabotage, Raider finally decided. He stifled a yawn behind his hand and took another swallow of the whiskey Welles provided.

Raider emptied his glass, and the little Chinese girl brought a bottle to refill it. "No thanks," Raider said, waving her away. He was so bored with this crap that he was not even interested in having another drink. That damned Kent's voice droned through the space of the salon like a blanket, snuffing out any pleasure Raider might have gotten from the quality of the whiskey.

He yawned again, not bothering to hide it this time, and thought about the quarters that had been given him.

When Kent had come down with the steam engine and string of flatcars, he had brought along, obviously on Welles's orders, a freight car that had been crudely converted for use as a sleeping coach. That car was now parked behind Welles's private luxury car. Raider, Doc, and presumably Kent had been given tiny sleeping rooms in the new car. Their gear had already been taken there by some of Welles's Chinese servants.

Piss on this, Raider thought. He stood and stretched.

Conversation in the salon halted, and everyone stared at him.

"It's been a long day," he said. "I'm gonna turn in now."

Welles shrugged. Kent went back to his interminable talk about the problems of laying rail in the mountains. Weatherbee gave him a questioning look, then returned his attention to the others.

Raider let himself out the back of the private car. He had to poke around in the closets off the vestibule to find his hat. Probably the little housegirl was supposed to do that for him, but she was busy fluttering attentively over Weatherbee's shoulder, which she had been doing most of the afternoon and evening. Whatever Doc had said to the dang girl, it seemed to have made an impression on her. She had been simpering all over him ever since.

Not that Raider gave a damn. Not this time. He was still having thoughts about that Wanda.

He smiled to himself as he stepped down off the rear platform and made his way carefully across the crushed rock of the roadbed toward the sleeping car. It was extremely dark, the night moonless, and he had to feel his way to avoid stumbling. The lights in the salon had been bright, and it would take some time before his eyes adjusted to the change.

He found the door in the side of the sleeping car and the small stepladder that had been placed there. There were no lanterns inside the car either, so he had to feel his way along the rough wood wall to the last sleeping compartment.

He closed the door behind him and felt his way to the narrow bunk that had been built against the wall. He remembered that there was a lamp hung on gimbals near the head of the bunk, but he did not bother to find and light it. He did not need to see in order to sleep.

Raider stretched again and yawned. He stripped off his things down to his smallclothes and dropped his gunbelt beside the bed. He sat on the edge of the bed, wishing briefly that he had had the foresight to bring a bottle with him. It was still pretty early. Not worth getting dressed again and going back to the other car for, though, he decided.

He shivered. It was chilly at this altitude, even though the calendar showed that fall should be several weeks away. Raider flipped back the hem of the heavy woolen blanket that lay over the bunk and crawled beneath the cover.

He stiffened, and his breath hissed through his teeth in surprise.

From the darkness very close to his ear he could hear a low chuckle.

It was already warm under the blanket. The warmth was that of flesh.

And now that he thought about it, he could identify his visitor by the light fragrance he remembered from lunch. The scent had been in his nostrils all afternoon in memory. Now it was here beside him.

He reached out a hand and encountered bare, warm, exceptionally soft skin.

Other fingers met his and guided his hand. They pressed his palm against the unmistakable swell of a large breast.

Raider grinned in the darkness.

Wanda pressed her body against his. She was naked. With practiced speed her hands fluttered over him, first determining what he might be wearing, then helping to relieve him of his underwear.

Her body was hot against his.

And her breath was hot, her lips eager, as she sought his mouth with hers. Her arms went around him. With one hand she stroked his back, then let the prowling hand drift south to his waist, then to his belly and in between them.

She gasped as she felt the length and the hardness of what she found there.

Once again he heard that low, soft murmur of chuckling sound in the night.

She pulled and clutched at him.

"Easy," he said. "You pull it off and ain't neither one of us gonna be satisfied."

Wanda laughed softly and wriggled flat on the narrow bunk. She must have been jammed uncomfortably against the side of the car to give him enough room to get into the small bunk before he discovered her presence there.

Raider raised himself to accommodate her, and she slid beneath him. When he lowered himself again he lay on a yielding mattress of womanflesh.

Wanda opened herself to him and guided him inside. Her sex was very wet and, in spite of his size, very loose.

Raider would have enjoyed an opportunity to touch and explore. To play with those magnificent breasts that he still had not really seen or had time to more than briefly feel.

But she seemed to be in a hurry. She was already moving. Pumping her hips under him.

The amount of her moisture and the loose, floppy size of her opening, however, kept him from getting much out of it. Although if he could accurately judge by the rate of Wanda's breathing, she was enjoying it a great deal.

Raider stopped the movements he had been automatically responding with. "Wait a second," he ordered. "Put your legs together."

She groaned a little, but she complied when he raised himself, first one leg and then the other, to allow her to bring her thighs together.

Now he lay completely on top of her, his knees outside of hers, with the hard length of his shaft still socketed inside her to join them.

Slowly he began to pump again. It was better this way. Her body had a firmer grip on him, and there was enough friction to give him some feeling.

Wanda began to grind her hips against his pelvis again, and he matched his rhythm to hers.

While she humped and withdrew under him, her hands raked back and forth across his back, her nails digging into his flesh more and more insistently.

After only a few moments her body stiffened and shuddered. Apparently she had already climaxed, although they had barely begun. Raider could not at the moment remember even having been with a woman before who was so quick on the trigger.

As soon as she had finished with her own pleasure, Wanda went limp under him.

She lay quiet and acquiescent as Raider pumped into her.

Ready as he had been to begin with, it took him several minutes to build up the interest he had thought he would have felt with this woman.

But after a time the pressure of flesh against sensitized flesh had the expected result. Raider began to plunge harder and faster, bucking and driving into her now until he gasped and lunged forward one last time, spewing a gout of hot fluid deep inside her.

He spent himself and, vaguely dissatisfied, rolled off her. Both had to turn sideways and lie belly to belly in order to remain together on the narrow bed.

Oddly, now that he was done, Wanda once again turned amorous, lacing her fingers behind his neck and pulling him to her for deep, tongue-probing kisses.

"You're so sweet. And so big. You do wonderful things to me, honey," she whispered. As far as he could recall it was the first time she had spoken to him since lunch.

She went on like that for a time, murmuring things that meant nothing. Praising him with extravagant compliments that he could not make himself believe.

She was licking his ear now, running the tip of her tongue—he would have welcomed some application of that tongue elsewhere a little while ago, but now found it only wet and, as quickly as she withdrew, chilly—and continuing to whisper and wheedle.

He paid little attention to her words, but after a time he realized—and was barely able to contain a bark of laughter—

that she was trying to plant ideas into the same ear she was slobbering over.

She kept saying something about how good he was, how good they were together, and how very good she would make it for him when he came back, when he had that huge, wonderful bonus Ruthie was going to pay him if only Raider would do the right thing and smash that Finch fellow, if only Raider would not mess around with investigations and slow stuff like that and go up there and get rid of that no-account Finch for Ruthie—and for her—because as soon as that was done Raider would have the bonus money and Raider and his adoring Wanda could be together, all Raider wanted, everything he could ever possibly want from a woman, and she was *so* anxious to give it to him, all of it, all of her, everything.

Raider withheld his laughter and let the fool woman do her job.

He almost shook his head, though. She really was not very good at this.

For that matter, he realized, great as she was to look at, Wanda was really not all that good at fucking either.

After a while, though, inevitably, her attentions began to have an effect on him. He began once again to rise to unwelcome attention.

Wanda felt the growing erection begin to press against her belly. She reached down to hold and touch him.

She tried once again to squirm beneath him.

"No," he said. "Roll over the other way."

"What?"

"I said—"

"You can't be serious."

"Of course I am. Roll over. You'll love it." Or someone would. It was, after all, most unlikely to be loose.

It would feel good, and, what the hell, he was hardly going to concern himself with what Wanda wanted.

She did as he directed. And after a few moments more Raider really did not give a damn what had brought her to his compartment.

CHAPTER SIX

Doc took a sip of his wine and wished he could pull out one of his own excellent Old Virginia cigars without offending Welles. The man had already offered cigars from a gold-chased humidor. The humidor was lovely, but the cigars it contained were of only slightly better quality than Judith's donkey dust would have been. Doc had already tried one of them. He did not want another.

The conversation in the salon waned. Sid Kent had been doing most of the talking the entire evening, and now the track crew foreman was too drunk to follow his own trains of thought, much less think or talk intelligently about how to get real trains moving.

"Have your men been doing anything to protect themselves or the road?" Doc asked. It was one of the things neither Welles nor Kent had gotten around to mentioning this evening. One of the few things.

"No," Welles said. "I got men up there that know what they're doing with an ax or a sledge or a . . . what do you call them things the survey crews use?"

"Theodolite," Doc said. He took another sip of the wine.

"Yeah. One o' them."

Doc wondered anew how T. Rutherford Welles, a man who seemed to have neither taste nor intelligence, had ever progressed so far.

"Anyway," Welles went on, "I got boys up there that can handle that shit. But none of them is any good with a gun. And o' course there's the Chinks. I got lots o' Chinks up there. But, hell, man, you can't give a gun to a Chinaman. No telling what the heathen monkeys might do." Welles laughed. He apparently thought he had made a joke.

Welles was quite oblivious to the fact that there was a "Chink" in the salon with them, patiently and pleasantly continuing to serve the same sorry son of a bitch who was demeaning her people.

Doc glanced at the girl in apology. Her expression showed nothing whatsoever, but he could not believe she would be able to listen to such comments without feeling resentment, regardless of whether she showed it. The girl's eyes met his for a fraction of a second, then slid quickly away. Doc felt embarrassment for her.

"That's why I called you boys in," Welles was saying. The huge man leaned forward in his chair, almost toppling out of it as he momentarily lost his balance. Apparently Welles was drunker than Doc had realized. Until then he had showed no signs of an evening of almost constant imbibing.

Welles recovered and laughed. He belched once and asked, "Mind if I ast you something, Weatherbee?"

"What would that be?"

"It's about, well, what we talked about earlier."

Doc raised an eyebrow.

"'Bout, you know, gettin' rid o' that prick Finch."

"I thought I had made it clear that—"

Welles waved a hand impatiently. "I know. You tol' me all that. You want to go by Pinkerton damn rules. 'S'awright, I guess. But what I was wondering . . . can a fella *really* hire men to . . . you know . . . do what he wants done?"

The question was much more answer than question as far as Doc was concerned. Ever since lunch he had been wondering why Rutherford Welles had hired the Pinkertons, even though he had worked with the agency before at the direction of smarter—and more decent—railroad executives. It would have been simpler for him, if criminally stupid of him, to go to Buena Vista or to Leadville beyond it and spend fifty dollars or so to hire someone more in line with Welles' crude manner of thinking.

Now that question had been answered. T. Rutherford Welles, wealthy and powerful and quick to gratify his own tastes and pleasures, simply had not known *how* to do such a thing.

"No," Doc lied. "Talk about things like that is just so much rumor."

Welles giggled and rocked sideways in his chair. "Yeah. I kinda thought it might be."

The big man's face suddenly went blank. He lost all expression and animation. He remained like that for only a moment, bolt upright in the overstuffed chair, then he slumped backward. He began to snore.

Doc looked at Sid Kent. The foreman too was pretty much out of it, reclining in his chair and making faint, babbling noises. This crowd could be a liquor salesman's dream account, Doc thought. Probably was, in fact. The labels on Welles's bottles were fancy and the prices therefore probably high, but the stuff was of inferior quality.

Doc got to his feet. Possibly the gentlemanly thing for a guest to do under such circumstances would be for him to carry Welles to his room. But Doc did not feel like being *that* much of a gentleman with Welles.

Besides, if Doc left him where he was, Welles could wake up with a drink already at hand. The imbecile would probably like that.

Doc headed for the door. He stopped at the vestibule, however, and turned back. The housegirl, tiny as she was, was struggling with Welles' inert body. The little woman was trying to haul him toward the front of the car with determination but with entirely too little strength. Welles likely outweighed her three and a half to one.

"Here," he said. "Don't try to do that alone."

She stopped what she was doing and looked at him. Doc was not sure but he thought he could see an unnatural, glistening brightness in her eyes, as if frustration—or something else—had brought her to the brink of tears.

"I must," the girl said. "The master would be very unhappy in the morning if I leave him here. I must put him to bed."

Doc nodded and left his hat where it was on the closet shelf. There would be time enough for it later. He crossed the floor of the salon to her side and bent over Welles.

Doc took a firm grip under the big man's arms and lifted. The girl tried without much success to help.

Weatherbee grunted with effort. Welles outweighed *him* by two to one.

Doc's physical strength was not as apparent as Raider's, but it was not lacking either. He was in excellent shape. He braced himself and tugged again, intending to lift Welles to his shoulder and carry him that way.

After a moment he gave up on that attempt. There are, after all, limits to every man's strength. And the utter limpness of Welles' huge form was simply too much to handle alone.

Doc quit trying to pick Welles up and settled for dragging the man instead. If the idiot's head bounced along the hallway, that would be just too, too bad.

The housegirl showed him the way through a wide door and down a hall.

There was only one bedroom built into the front of the private car. It was quite as large as the salon area, with one end blocked off for a closet and a small crapper.

The sleeping chamber was decorated as ornately as the rest of the car, with a broad, canopied bed and, in one end of the room, an oversize brass tub for bathing.

Doc sniffed the fetid air in the closed bedroom and wondered why Welles would ever have bothered to install a tub. Judging from the odors in the air there, he seldom if ever used the thing.

The bed, handsome though it was, was rumpled and sour smelling. The sheets looked like they had not been changed since the car was put into use.

Doc wrinkled his nose and dragged Welles to the side of the big bed. He lifted mightily under the man's arms, and the little housegirl helped. Between them they were able to pick Welles up high enough to dump him onto the bed. The girl bent over her employer and began removing his clothes.

Doc stood in the doorway and waited for her. He had no clear reason for doing so but felt a remote impulse to do something, say something that might assure her that not all Occidental males were like T. Rutherford Welles. He was still feeling embarrassed for her.

The sight of the naked Welles was hardly Doc's idea of masculine good looks. The man's belly was a mountain of blue-veined wrinkles, his skin the mottled, blotchy color of a dead fish.

The girl seemed quite familiar with her chore. She removed his clothing and tucked his feet and arms into a natural sleeping position, then pulled the soiled sheet up to his chest.

When she was done she turned and came to stand in front of Doc. She bowed to him, very low, and said something in her own language. She said it, whatever it was, slowly and with an air of great formality.

Doc had no idea what the hell he should say in return. Instead he returned her bow.

The girl smiled when she straightened. "May I have the honor of lighting your way, sir?"

His first inclination was to refuse the offer. Then he realized. The offer was of thanks, not just politeness. "You're very kind," he said. "Thank you."

She beamed with pleasure and ran lightly down the hall to fetch a lantern. She lighted it and led the way out of the fancy car, stopping to get Doc's pearl gray derby and taking time to carefully brush it before she presented it to him. Then she took him out into the night and lighted his path to the sleeping car Kent had brought down with the work train.

Doc's sleeping compartment and Raider's were at opposite ends of the car. The housegirl lighted his way to the door of the tiny compartment and then went inside to use a wisp of straw to transfer flame from her lantern to the lamp that was mounted on the wall by his bed.

She bowed to him again.

"Thank you, Miss . . . I'm sorry. I don't even know your name."

He might have said more, but he stopped, astounded. The girl was crying. Fat, elongated teardrops were rolling down her cheeks, leaving behind wet tracks that caught the lamplight and gleamed.

Instinctively Doc Weatherbee reached out to stroke her cheek and neck and the back of her head, trying to sooth and comfort her.

He pulled her to him and wrapped his arms around her, petting her shoulders and back.

He crooned to her as he stroked her, words, sounds that had meaning more in what they intended than in what they said. She was trembling under his touch.

After a few moments in which she gave herself limply

to his touch, she stiffened and jerked back away from him.

"It's all right," Doc assured her. "I don't intend to . . . take advantage of you."

Damned if she did not begin to cry all over again. And this time she flung herself forward into his arms of her own volition.

CHAPTER SEVEN

Her name was Kwan Mei-lin. She was ashamed of herself.
Her conduct was not proper. She apologized over and over
again while Doc tried to comfort her, tried to explain that
she had done nothing remotely wrong.

It was just that it had been so long since anyone, of any
race, had been so very kind to her. She had forgotten herself,
forgotten her lowly position. She tried again to apologize.

No, she did not work for Rutherford Welles. She had no
choice about being here.

The cretinous bastard owned her.

Doc's eyes flashed cold fire, but he did not let the still
weeping girl realize his anger as he tried to assimilate what
she was telling him.

Welles had bought her when she was very young—nine
or ten years old, she thought. She believed she was now
about twenty-two. She was not sure of that.

Her countrymen, those who worked for Welles, were employees, not slaves. Kwan Mei-lin was beneath them. Besides, she had been with the foreign devil so long that she spoke like one, her Chinese was terrible. And they said she smelled like a foreign devil too. They wanted nothing to do with her.

No one wanted anything to do with her. Except Welles. And that was rare nowadays. He had become tired of her over the years.

She had no value.

She was not worthy of the kind man's sympathies and generosity.

She apologized.

Doc continued to hold and stroke her. He knew of no words he could use that might convince her that she was a person with any value, much less that she was a human being with rights of her own.

As he held her, so very small against him, with her tears saturating his shirt barely at chest level, he began to feel an unwelcome arousal prompted by her nearness and her warmth. He tried to twist aside so that she would not become aware of it.

Kwan Mei-lin pressed herself all the tighter against him, and his effort was in vain.

That, oddly, was what finally calmed her and allowed her to quit crying.

It was, he guessed, both something she knew how to handle and at the same time a gift she could give him in repayment for something she obviously thought to be a great kindness.

The girl—she was so small that he continued to think of her as still a girl, although she had said she thought she was into her twenties—calmed and began to rub herself deliberately and provocatively against him.

He resisted her at first. "That isn't necessary," he tried to explain. "I didn't have that in mind. I really didn't."

"I believe you," she whispered to him. "But please. Let me relieve you. I am worthless, but this I can do. Please."

She was looking up at him, her tiny body pressed against his. Her face was very small, and she seemed heart-breakingly vulnerable.

Doc bent and kissed her. He did it gently. The girl began to weep again but very softly this time.

"What's wrong?" he asked.

"No one has ever kissed me before."

"Never?" He was astonished.

"No, never. I have been used, yes. Many times. Many years. No one has ever kissed me."

Doc wanted to weep for her. He could not truly comprehend the type of life that had been hers.

He kissed her again. Tentatively, obviously uncertain of how this should be done, Kwan Mei-lin's lips parted and she kissed him back. Her shy and unknowing response gave her an innocence that was touching.

It was also, in a way, inflammatory. It heightened his feelings for her, made him want to protect her. But made him want her all the more at the same time.

He probed the inside of her mouth with his tongue. A moment later he felt the dart of her tongue flickering hesitantly into his mouth. She explored the idea of it, then accepted it and began with a virginal eagerness to kiss him deeply.

He found his hands moving over her body, quite of their own will. He had not intended to do that, but he found himself touching her anyway.

Kwan Mei-lin shifted to allow him access to her form.

She was small, slim as a willow withe. That had been obvious to begin with.

But the loose, baggy clothing of her station had hidden from him an unexpected treasure.

Her breasts were as small and as delicate as rosebuds, her nipples tiny, hard tips on those soft buds.

Her waist was impossibly narrow. He was sure he could encircle it with his hands.

That, he knew, was an expression, a description, but never a real possibility.

On an impulse, Doc dropped his hands to her waist. He was able to touch thumbtip to thumbtip at her navel. Behind her back—so sleek and smooth—he was able to press the tip of one middle finger against the other.

Incredible, he thought.

He had his hands beneath the hem of her loose jacket now. Her flesh was cool to his touch. It felt like satin. He ran his left hand up her side, each individual rib clearly felt under a paper-thin covering of taut skin. The touch must have tickled. She giggled involuntarily and pulled away from him.

She was laughing, and Doc laughed with her.

Kwan Mei-lin stepped backward another pace and grasped the bottom edge of her jacket. In one swift, fluid motion she pulled it up over her head and cast it aside.

She untied a cord at her waist and let her trousers drop to the floor around her ankles.

Her body was lovely, a pale, creamy bronze color, not at all the yellow that her people were said to be.

Her nipples were very dark, with practically no areolae surrounding them.

She had a dense, curly patch of jet hair at the vee between her thighs.

Doc smiled and stood there for a moment, wanting just to enjoy the look of her. She seemed to understand his desire. She stood patiently, waiting for him to finish.

Her body, small as it was, was delightfully proportioned. She was a Venus in miniature, only a slight shortness in her legs—in the length of her thighs, actually—marring the ideal proportions.

After a moment Doc nodded. His pleasure and his approval were obvious in his expression.

Kwan Mei-lin smiled and stepped out of one leg of her trousers, using the toe of her other foot to toss the garment aside.

She posed there for another few seconds, then moved closer to him.

Quickly, with a light, sure touch, she unbuttoned his shirt and helped him out of it, then knelt.

She bent low and helped him off with his spats and shoes and stockings. He dropped his trousers, and she swept them aside. He stood naked above her, his arousal shouting his need in the bouncing hardness of his erection. With every heartbeat of fresh blood-flow the tip of his cock bumped upward.

Doc was embarrassed by what Kwan Mei-lin did next. He might have anticipated, even welcomed, anything else.

She shuffled back away from him on her knees, then bowed low, continuing down and forward until her forehead was pressed against the tops of his feet.

It was an act of total submission, of total obeisance.

She straightened, still on her knees, and took his hand, turning him and guiding him down onto the bed beside her.

He sat, then allowed her to press him down flat on his back. He was lying on the bed with Kwan Mei-lin kneeling at his side.

She bent over him to kiss his mouth, then his chest. She ran her tongue slowly, barely touching him, around and over each of his nipples.

She rocked back on her heels. For a moment he did not know what she was doing. Then he saw that she was undoing the tight braids of her hair.

When she was done, the pigtail that had fallen to her waist now extended well below her buttocks. She pulled the twin cascades of hair around in front so that they fell over her breasts. With her fingers she quickly brushed them out as best she could.

She moved over him, sweeping the curling ends of her

hair up and down his body. The feel of it was tantalizing.

She bent over his groin, using her dangling hair to tease and titillate his erection.

Then she lowered herself to him. The cool, light touch of her hair spilled down over his scrotum.

He could feel her breath, warm and faintly moist, on the head of his cock. She parted her lips and poised just above him, deliberately teasing him with her breath.

Then, when he thought he could not hold still any longer without having to grab her and force her to *do* something, Kwan Mei-lin dipped her head lower.

Her tongue darted and lashed, danced and flickered. The contacts were everywhere at once, light and then fierce, hot and then so faint they might have been imagined. Over and into the small slit in the end of his cock, around and around the engorged bulb of its head, covering every bit of surface along his shaft, down to his balls and back again.

He began to writhe under her touch, the constant changes of pace and place and intensity driving him almost beyond control.

When he thought he could take no more, not a single second longer, Kwan Mei-lin paused.

She bent lower, opening her mouth and extending her jaw as she did so, encircling him, dropping lower and lower over him until she covered the head of his cock completely but not allowing any part of herself to touch him until the head was fully inside her mouth.

Then, gently, she pressed her lips around the head, holding him with a firm, insistent grip.

She began to suckle him. Lightly at first and then harder, harder still, until the pull of her mouth was almost painful.

She came off her knees and raised her slim body over him positioning herself exactly where she wished to be.

Still sucking on him, she pressed down, lowering her mouth over him, the grasp of her lips hot and hard around him. She pushed, down, deeper.

He could feel the resistance at the back of her mouth as he reached the opening of her throat.

Still she pushed, pressing against him, driving herself down on him harder and harder.

She continued to push, forcing him past that restrictive ring until his cock entered the throat passage itself.

She took all of him, all of his shaft, completely into her mouth and throat until he could feel her upper lip against his balls and the point of her chin was pushing painfully against his stomach at the base of his cock.

Doc groaned. His hips began to quiver and pulsate with a desire to stroke into her like that, but he did not want to chance hurting her. She was so very small that he was afraid of what he might do if he let himself go and acted on the impulses that were flooding through him now.

Mei-lin seemed to understand the needs in him. She backed off, only by fractions of an inch at first, then more, each time she withdrew driving back down upon him, bobbing her head, her entire upper body, to accomplish the strokes he did not feel he dared make.

An exquisite pressure built deep in his groin, building with all the overwhelming force of steam in a closed container, until he could stand it no longer, until he could hold back no more.

With a cry of loud release, Doc exploded.

Mei-lin tightened the grip of her lips around the base of him. Her hold on him there slowed and heightened the sensations he was given. The surging flow of his climax felt like it would never end.

Nor did he want it to.

Eventually, though, it did. It was just as well that it did, he thought. No one could stand that kind of sustained release without his heart bursting. The pleasure had been almost too much to bear. Almost, but not quite.

Even then Mei-lin stayed with him, continued to hold him deep inside her.

Very slowly, still sucking, she raised her head from him, allowing him to slip free bit by bit until she held just the tip of him within a light grasp of her lips.

She let him go then with a sigh.

Doc was limp. And not just at his crotch. He felt limp and relaxed, totally and utterly spent, flaccid to the very marrow of his bones. If he had had to get up off the bed and walk at that moment, he was sure he could not possibly have done so.

He smiled and weakly raised a hand to stroke the golden satin of her hip.

He slid his other hand across the firm, flat planes of her belly and fondled first one breast and then the other. Her nipples were still as hard as bone. She was still in a state of arousal, even though he had been completely satiated.

He would have to do something about that.

She was still kneeling on the edge of the bed, her head above his crotch, her belly over his chest.

He put his hands around that impossibly small waist and pulled her to him, bringing her into position above him. And then down.

She was clean, and her flesh had a faintly sweet flavor.

Mei-lin opened herself to him and began to moan and writhe at his touch as he brought her higher and higher toward an explosion of immensely powerful release.

When he was done, Mei-lin cried again. But this time Doc did not worry about her tears. This time he did not have to try to soothe them away.

He smiled and took her hand, drawing her to him until she lay pressed tight against him, her face in the hollow of his throat, her breathing a welcome warmth against his skin.

Mei-lin sighed. "I have never been so happy," she whispered.

"Thank you," he said. "I could not possibly think of a finer compliment, Mei-lin. Thank you."

She smile and sighed and kissed him, gently this time, without urgency.

Her presence against him, her very obvious joy at being with him, were very nice indeed, Doc thought.

He closed his eyes and let himself drift toward sleep.

The lamp and the lantern were still burning. He did not care. He felt a drowsy lassitude that made movement to extinguish them beneath thought.

Mei-lin's breathing told him that she was already asleep. And quickly he joined her.

CHAPTER EIGHT

Doc withdrew from her with a sigh of deep satisfaction and stood, groping for his clothes and the first smoke of the morning. It was just now coming dawn, but already they had been awake for more than an hour. Weatherbee would have enjoyed spending more time with the delightful Chinese, but she was terrified of the thought of being late to her duties.

Even so she took the time to help him dress—a form of assistance that first shocked and then faintly amused him—before she pulled on her own two garments.

Kwan Mei-lin knelt in front of Weatherbee and took his hand in hers, turning it so she could press her lips to his palm. The gesture was embarrassing.

She looked up at him, her dark eyes serious now. She looked worried.

She hesitated for a moment, then in a small, halting voice

said, "Do not go to the camps. They may not be safe for you. For any white man."

Mei-lin rose and tried to hurry from the room, but Doc clamped his hand around her wrist. "Why?" he asked.

She looked frightened. "I should not have spoken," she said in a whisper. "But you are such a good man . . ."

"What is it, Mei-lin?" he asked gently.

Mei-lin dropped her eyes from his and turned her head away. She was small and childlike in her vulnerability. Doc pulled her closer and held her, trying to comfort her. But he had to know what she meant by those few words of warning. "What is it?" he asked again.

"The master," she said, looking first to reassure herself that the door was closed, that there was no one to overhear.

"Welles? What about him?"

"I . . . I hear things," Mei-lin said. "The people ignore me, but I hear things. In the master's car. And in the other, where the servants stay. You know?"

He nodded.

"Always before, when they were paid by others, the men received what they were promised. Not so now."

"What do you mean?"

"The master, he is running out of money. He spends for his own needs. He pays his white foremen and work leaders. I know this. I have seen him give them money. But the Chinese he pays with promises. For weeks now. He gives them a little food, tells his men to explain they will all be paid at once when the job is done. The men are having doubts. There is talk . . ." She apparently could not go on.

"They might walk off the job?" Doc prompted.

Mei-lin looked at him with confusion in her eyes. "They could not do that," she said.

It was Doc's turn to be confused. "Why not?"

"They all know. If they leave an agreement before it is complete, they have no right to return home. The laws. They all know."

"Do you mean they think the United States government would prevent them from returning to China if they walk off a job?" Doc asked.

"Of course," Mei-lin said with complete conviction. "I was there. I heard the master explain this to them."

"Even if they weren't being paid for the job?"

"The laws belong to the white men. And the master says he is not failing to pay them, only delaying the pay."

"Jesus!" Doc said. He hadn't had any respect for Welles to begin with, so it wouldn't really be possible for him to lose respect for the man. But this ... He shook his head. "You told me to stay away from the camps, Mei-lin. If the men are so angry but can't walk off their jobs, what are they going to do?"

"I do not know. Truly I do not, or I would tell you. But I know how it is. I have felt the loss of home already. I have felt the same things. If I were a better and stronger person I would already have done what I think they will do."

"What is that, Mei-lin?"

"If they cannot return home someday with money to care for the families they left there, their spirits can return. No law can separate a man's spirit from those of his ancestors."

Doc felt a cold shiver race up his spine. "They would all kill themselves?"

"Oh, no," Mei-lin said, obviously upset by the thought of mass suicide. "That would not be honorable. No, they would go to the hatchet and the ax. The white men would kill them, of course. Those white men who were not killed themselves. But it would all be honorable. Then the men's spirits could return and join their ancestors at home, where they belong." Mei-lin sounded like it was all perfectly logical and simple.

"Jesus," Weatherbee said again.

"I have to go now. Please."

Doc nodded. He bent low and gave her a kiss, then

released her. She slipped out the door so quietly he could not have heard her if his back had been turned—a slim, small wraith in a white linen jacket and baggy trousers.

Doc found the cigar he had been wanting and lighted it. He sat on the edge of the bunk that was still warm and softly scented from Mei-lin's presence.

This complication was not a part of the assignment the Pinkerton Agency had given them. But damn!

CHAPTER NINE

End-of-track was less than seven miles west of the siding where T. Rutherford Welles lounged in tipsy luxury in his private car. The work of laying more rails, despite Sid Kent's endless talk the night before, did not seem to be going all that rapidly.

Raider turned to Doc and said, "They don't seem to have all that big a stockpile of steel, do they?"

"No," Weatherbee said, "and I didn't see any waiting back at the D&RG end either."

"Delivery delay?" Raider suggested.

Doc grunted but did not answer. Raider knew what Weatherbee would be thinking about—what that Chinese girl had told him this morning. Doc had relayed it to Raider on the way up in the freight car. Along with the horses. Doc had been pissed about having to ride in a car with the livestock, but there were no passenger cars on the few miles of track laid to date.

In fact, unless an awful lot of freights and flatcars had been taken back toward the river last night with the work train that had brought Kent down, Welles owned damned little rolling stock of any kind. Likely just the one narrow gauge engine and a handful of flats, perhaps a pair of freight cars, and of course Welles' fancy shit.

It seemed, Raider thought, like a helluva poor way to run a railroad. But then, he was willing to admit that he didn't know a whole lot about running railroads. Or building them.

Certainly someone up here seemed to know what he was doing. Beyond the line of brand-new steel rails gleaming in the sun, the roadbed stretched out of sight toward the now not very distant mountains.

Square, creosoted ties were laid far in advance of the steel, laid in an orderly pattern on a smooth, level roadbed built of packed gravel and finely broken rock. A hell of a lot of work had gone into the crushing and laying of the ballast for the bed.

There were fewer laborers in view than Raider would have expected. He had heard the glory stories about the laying of the transcontinental connection, the Union Pacific building from one end, the Central Pacific from the other, thousands of men marching forward at rates of several miles a day, laying steel and driving spikes in a frenzy of activity. The old-timers who had seen that sight still talked about it with pride and awe.

This was . . . nothing remotely like that.

While Raider watched, a dozen stocky, bare-backed, sweating Chinese picked up a rail and lugged it into place.

A white man knelt on the prickly gravel and took his time about positioning the steel just so on top of the already emplaced ties.

Then the Chinese, some of the same men who had just carried the rail into place, took up hammers and spikes and began to set the steel.

While they worked, a group of whites, whose function here Raider could not begin to understand, stood with folded arms and watched them.

Now that Kent was back . . . , he thought. But the foreman only went over to the lounging whites and began to talk with them. The Chinese laborers Kent virtually ignored.

"What do you think, Doc?"

Weatherbee shook his head. He didn't look happy. "I truly hate to admit it, Rade, but I think we should adopt your suggestion. At least until we see who and what is up there." Weatherbee motioned with his chin toward the imposing peaks that loomed nearly straight up from here.

As if he had been thinking the same thing Raider was, Weatherbee added, "It should be interesting to see how they've managed to find a negotiable grade over those mountains. From here it looks impossible."

Raider ignored the distraction and returned to Doc's first point. "You agree, then. We go in an' poke around some. Mix in without tellin' anyone what we're doing."

Weatherbee sighed. "I agree."

"You c'n take on this Finch fella. I'll take a look at the workin' stiffs."

Doc nodded, offering no argument. "All right."

"What the hell's the matter with you this morning?" Raider asked.

"Nothing. Why?"

Raider shrugged. "It ain't like you, going along with somethin' sensible. That ain't like you at all."

"You said it yourself, Rade. The plan is sensible. I investigate the offices, where intelligence may be required, and you remain in the stables."

The little son of a bitch didn't even smile when he said it. Something was definitely bothering him.

Raider did not rise to the bait, though, which may have been what that damned Weatherbee intended after all. A man never quite knew with him. Weatherbee sometimes could stand there looking serious as an undertaker and still be pulling a fellow's leg.

"All right, then," Raider said. "We split before we get to Tincup. Go in separate, and if you see me you make like you don't know me."

"That," Doc said, "will be easy to accomplish. And a pleasure."

Raider grunted and swung onto his roan. If Doc wanted to split now, it was all right with him.

"Do you have any plans for meeting to pool our information?" Weatherbee asked.

"Nope."

"Don't you think we should?"

"It'll work out," Raider told him. "Don't be so damn set in your ways, Doc. Let things happen."

Weatherbee looked annoyed. "Procedure calls for—"

"Procedure's a bunch of shit," Raider interrupted. Before Doc could say anything more, Raider kneed the roan into motion. He glanced over his shoulder. Weatherbee was still standing beside the tall, handsome, damned near useless bay horse. Doc was trying to get into the saddle, but the bay was not cooperating. It kept trying to spin away from him.

Raider chuckled. Weatherbee was going to have to cheek the critter down in order to get onto it. And by then Raider would be halfway to Tincup. Raider bumped the horse into a lope, drawing farther ahead before Doc would have time to mount.

Raider topped Tincup Pass late in the afternoon and stopped there to let the horse blow.

It seemed incredible to him that anyone could hope to bring a rail line up here, that the grades could be made slight enough for the road to be feasible, but damned if the tortuously winding bed had not been pretty much prepared already to within a few miles of the pass summit. Of course it was in these last few miles that the tricky parts would come.

The expensive ones too, he realized. There would have to be some tunnel work done. He didn't see how it could be otherwise.

Behind him Raider had already passed a number of camps and work crews. The Chinese laborers were abundant up here where the hard part of the work was being done. The men labored with hand tools. They used shovels and buckets instead of scrapers; rakes and the butt ends of logs instead of rollers or crushers to grade the path and pack the gravel. Others of them used heavy sledges to create gravel where none was conveniently available.

The whole damn country up here was rock. Or a clear majority of it, if not quite all. Welles' powder costs for the blasting must be enormous, Raider thought.

But the view from the top of the pass was exceptional. It was like a man could see to the ends of the earth. Raider had no idea what the elevation was up here, but the top of Tincup Pass was virtually at timberline. The peaks that rose even higher around him showed nothing but weather-shattered rock and deep drifts of snow. Those peaks marched in all directions from here, rank after rank of them, like waves in the sea. Below and behind him the wide beauty of the Arkansas River valley seemed like little more than a wrinkle in the earth.

Below and before him Raider could see the sparkling blue glint of a mountain lake, and beyond that, columns of smoke that would almost surely indicate the town of Tincup. A road of sorts, too narrow for wagon traffic, the same one he had been following ever since he left the last of Welles' work crews behind, led down past the lake toward the town.

Raider nudged the roan into motion again, slower this time, letting the animal pick its way across a sloping flat of slick rock until its hoofs once again touched soil and would have a better purchase. Man and horse could take a

nasty fall on rock under the best of conditions. What the
road must be like in the winter, with ice and packed snow
adding to the difficulties of the footing, Raider did not even
want to know.

He rode down slowly, once again reaching the dark timber where huge firs and a few stunted junipers grew. Strands
of aspen mixed here and there among the firs, their trunks
white and their foliage brighter. Some of the aspens had
already begun to pale, he noticed, reminding him that snow
could come now at any time. And within a month or two
the winter would set in. Within a few weeks the aspen leaves
would turn a shimmering gold and then would be gone.
Raider hoped he wouldn't still be here when the first of the
snows came. Getting out—or getting a work crew up—
could be a hell of a problem once that happened.

He turned in his saddle, thinking about the Chinese struggling to reach this point, and wondered if Welles had made
provision for them during the winter. All Raider had seen
in the camps he passed had been tents. And tents would be
the same as no protection at all once the wind-driven snows
arrived.

He could no longer see them, of course. The roan was
well below the summit of Tincup Pass now. Behind him he
could see only stone and sky. Before him he could foresee
only problems.

He rode on down, splashing through the creek of cold,
melting old snow that fed the clear, mirrorlike lake and then
beyond, until he could see the town laid out below him.

It was larger than he had expected, containing probably
more than a thousand people. The white steeple of a church
projected upward in the center of Tincup. Around it were
row upon row of small, tight cabins.

Raider grunted to himself, and the roan's ears flicked
back in response to the sound.

"Easy, old boy," he said softly. "You're fixing to get your
rest."

CHAPTER TEN

Doc Weatherbee found the headquarters of the Finch Freight and Transfer Company without difficulty. In fact, the complex of buildings and corrals would have been difficult to miss.

An office building, stables, equipment storage sheds, harness and blacksmith shops, and a series of stoutly fenced pens and small pastures were laid out on a broad, grassy flat at the south end of town. It was, Doc had to admit, an impressive operation.

Doc plow-reined the idiot bay into the rutted, much traveled drive leading off the Cumberland Pass road and stopped the horse by riding him head-on into the east wall of the office building. The tactic was, he had discovered, the most efficient way to halt the beast.

A number of men were relaxing in the late afternoon sunlight nearby. Probably employees who had finished their work and were waiting for others to join them. Without exception the loungers Doc could see were well-set-up men heavy with muscle and heavily armed. They looked like a rough crowd. They displayed no hostility toward him, though. They were rough but not belligerent.

"Good-looking horse," one of them commented with a grin.

"If he were mine you could have him," Doc answered with a smile as he gratefully dismounted. Getting the sorry creature over Tincup Pass had been a trial.

"And if he was mine," the freighter said, "I reckon I'd shoot him."

Doc led the stupid animal to a handy rail—miserable as the bay was to ride, it was docile and well-mannered when being led—and tied it there. "Is Mr. Finch available?" Doc asked the man who had spoken with him.

The freighter shrugged. "This ain't my day to keep track of him, but you can ask inside."

Doc thanked the man and went into the office.

The headquarters building was constructed like every-thing else in Tincup. Stoutly. It was built of thick timbers and was low to the ground with a sloping roof to keep the weight of the winter snows from collapsing it.

The interior was crudely furnished but seemed efficient enough. A low railing separated the public area from desks where office workers took care of dispatching, billing, and whatever. Benches were provided in the public section where potential customers could wait. One desk had been set facing the rail. A reception clerk sat there. The other desks were occupied, but no one paid any attention to Doc's arrival except for the clerk.

"Can I help you?" the man asked.

"Please," Doc said. "I would like to see Mr. Finch."

"We have a traffic manager who can arrange shipment of anything you want, sir," the clerk said.

Doc shook his head. "This is about something else."

"Just a minute then." The clerk left his desk and went

to a doorway leading into a separate room on the left end of the long, low building. He was back within moments. "Mr. Finch has someone with him now. He'll be free in a bit."

"I can wait," Doc said. He removed his derby and settled onto one of the benches. Within five minutes or so a man came out of the office carrying a sheaf of papers. He went to one of the desks in the big room, spread the papers out in front of him, and began transferring figures from them onto a ledger.

"Sir?" the clerk asked.

"Yes."

"Mr. Finch is free now."

The clerk opened a small gate in the railing and held it for Doc to pass through, then showed him the way to Finch's private office.

Corey Finch was a man in his late thirties or early forties. He was taller and more heavily built than Doc, and there was no fat on him. He looked like a man who might have gotten his start through hard labor and persistence, but he was no bumpkin who had achieved success through luck. He was quite obviously bright enough to be the creative force behind the efficiency Doc had noted in the outer office.

Finch was wearing a smartly tailored business suit, its coat hung on a standing rack behind his desk, his shirtsleeves gartered now and his desk cluttered with invoices and way-bills.

He was not a handsome man, but he seemed a pleasant enough sort. When he looked up from his papers to welcome his visitor, Doc's impression was one of intelligence and honesty.

"Yes?"

Doc shook the man's hand and introduced himself. Finch offered him a chair and asked, "What may I do for you, Mr. Weatherbee?"

Doc had not been sure until this moment of how he would

approach Corey Finch. Now, on the spur of the moment, he pulled out his wallet and opened it to his Pinkerton identification.

There was neither alarm nor hesitation in Finch's response. The man examined the credentials and handed the wallet back to Doc. "Yes?" he repeated.

"I assume you know why I'm here," Doc said.

Finch frowned. "If I had to make an assumption, sir, I would say that one of my customers has contacted your, uh, agency about the robberies. Although I have assured all of them that our insurance coverage is more than adequate to protect them." Then Finch smiled. "But of course. That's it, isn't it? The insurance company has hired the Pinkerton Agency. Good. Believe me, Mr. Weatherbee, I will do anything I can to cooperate in your investigation."

"Thank you," Doc said, not correcting the misunderstanding. He had no idea what Finch was talking about, but he was willing to listen. Particularly if the information might shed some light on the problems of T. Rutherford Welles' railroad.

"Is there anything in particular you wanted to know, Mr. Weatherbee?" Finch asked.

"What I would like you to do, Mr. Finch, is explain the situation to me. Right from the top."

"Of course." Finch pulled a watch in a gold hunt case from his vest pocket and opened it. "It's nearly quitting time," he said, "and this may take a while. Would you rather we do it over dinner and drinks?"

"If you prefer."

"Good," Finch said with a smile. "My wife will be expecting me, and I'm sure she won't mind a guest for supper. There isn't a decent hotel in Tincup yet."

"You are very kind, sir."

"Not at all," Finch said. "Glad to do it." He stood and shuffled together some of the papers on his desk, setting them aside and then putting the rest into a pile that he carried into the outer office and gave to one of the men working there. "Check these, Henry, to make sure they're accurate, then pass them along to Warren for payment, if you don't mind."

Finch got his coat and hat and motioned for Doc to join him. He led the way outside.

The sun was going down over the mountains to the west, and there was a sharp nip in the air. "I walk to and from work, Mr. Weatherbee. Hope you don't mind."

"Not at all, but I have a rented horse here." Doc pointed toward the miserable bay waiting patiently at the rail.

"We can put him up here for you. The care won't be any worse than at the livery in town."

Doc thanked him, and Finch called to one of the men in the yard. "Bud, ask Gerry to take care of this horse for Mr. Weatherbee, would you?"

"Sure thing, Corey."

"The horse will be available any time you want him, day or night," Finch said. "We have a very efficient staff of hostlers to take care of our stock. I insist on it. We couldn't hope to operate without our draft stock, you see."

"Of course," Doc said. He followed Finch on the short walk to the man's house, which was a little larger than most of those around it but otherwise was unpretentious.

Mrs. Finch was a plain woman a few years younger than her husband. She expressed no disapproval at the arrival of an unexpected guest but gave Doc a warm welcome and rose on her tiptoes to give Finch a kiss of greeting. "Supper will be ready in three quarters of an hour, gentlemen," she said. She went off toward the back of the house, and Finch took Doc into their small parlor. He poured two glasses of whiskey and gave one to Weatherbee. They were seated in overstuffed chairs, surrounded by the crowded, homey atmosphere of many years of married life. The home seemed a comfortable one.

"Now, sir, what can I tell you?"

"Everything, if you don't mind," Doc said. He was beginning to feel like something of a serpent, coming into this home on false pretenses.

Damn it all, he *liked* Corey Finch and his plain but quite obviously much loved missus.

Doc reminded himself firmly that he was here to do a job, though. And that job was to find out who was behind the sabotage of the AVT&P railroad. The job had *nothing* to do with Doc's personal opinions about T. Rutherford Welles or Mr. and Mrs. Corey Finch.

He suspected he might have to issue that reminder to himself frequently until this case was solved.

CHAPTER ELEVEN

Raider found a hotel and checked in. There were three to choose from in Tincup. One looked to be about as bad as the next. Raider made his choice based on its nearness to the most decent-looking of the town's dozen or so saloons. He left the roan at the livery on the north end of town and ate supper at a café that catered to the miners who formed the basis for Tincup's existence. Diners in the café shared the long tables and either ate what was served or went elsewhere for their meal. There was no menu.

Raider found a place at one of the tables and accepted a clean cup and bowl from the man who took his money. Pots of coffee and serving bowls of stew were placed at intervals along the table. Raider helped himself. The stew wasn't bad.

The man next to him pushed his empty bowl away and lighted a pipe. The aroma of the tobacco wasn't nearly as bad as those stinking things Weatherbee smoked.

"Been here long?" Raider asked the man.

"Ayuh. Some. You?"

"Just got in," Raider told him.

"If you're lookin' for a claim, good luck."

"Most of them taken, are they?"

"Ayuh. Most worth having."

"Small outfits around here, I noticed."

The miner nodded. "Everywhere you look. Can't hardly take a step without falling in somebody's shaft or tripping over a prospect hole."

"Decent folk around here?"

"I've seen worse."

The café man came around with a plate of biscuits, and Raider helped himself to several, breaking one into halves and using it to sop some of the thick gravy that was part of the stew. "Any big outfits in the district yet?" he asked the miner.

"None that'd be called big anywheres else. A few big enough to want to hire, if that's what you're looking for."

"Not really," Raider said. He took a swallow of nearly cold coffee and made a face. It tasted bitter. "I suppose the district will grow considerable when the railroad gets here."

The miner shrugged. "Some, I expect, but this is mostly small-claim country. The ore pays out all right. Be some better *if* the railroad gets here."

"Why is that?"

"Cheaper haulage," the man said. "That'll mean better profit for them as has some ore to ship. Cheaper goods, too, on the stuff comin' in. Better all the way around."

"So I'd expect you ought to want to see the rails get here," Raider said. "But a minute ago you sounded like you didn't think that would happen."

"That's because I don't think it will," the miner said.

"Why?"

"You just got here. I been for a spell. Wait till you see the first winter up this way, then ask me that again."

"That bad, huh?"

"Worse'n that bad. Ass deep to a high horse is just the start of it. Besides, everybody knows that that Welles fella is an asshole. He'll go broke before he ever gets his steel laid halfway."

"Everybody knows that, huh?"

"Ayuh. Everybody does."

"Can you think of anybody who'd want to see the railroad go broke?"

The miner shook his head. "Nope. Be better for us all if they made it. But they won't."

"What about the freight outfit that's getting all the hauling business now?"

The miner shrugged. "Far as I know, they don't have nothing to worry about, so they ain't particularly worrying about it."

"Interesting," Raider said.

"If you say so." The miner swiveled around on the single bench that served that side of the table, jammed the stem of his pipe between his teeth, and left without saying good-bye.

Raider returned to his meal.

Later he stopped in at the saloon long enough to have a few drinks and to find out that this was not his night to make a killing at the roulette wheel. The place was being worked by a handful of exceptionally ugly whores, most of whom looked like they'd have to be deloused before they'd be safe to get close to. Raider had a final snort and went back to his hotel.

He collected his key from the desk man and headed toward the back of the sprawling, one-floor structure.

"Well," he said. "Fancy meeting you here."

Doc Weatherbee was standing in front of one of the doors on the corridor, obviously having some difficulty with the lock.

Weatherbee glanced up and down the hall. It was empty.

He managed to get the door open and motioned Raider inside.

"I told you it'd work out that we could meet," Raider said. He helped himself to a seat on Doc's sagging bed and reached for his partner's flask of brandy on the bedside table.

"I suppose you have the case all wrapped up by now," Doc said.

"'Bout as close to it as you are, I'd expect. Or closer."

"Then you don't have to have learned much."

"Find out anything?" Raider asked.

"Nothing that would help, I can tell you that. In fact, quite the opposite."

"How's that?"

"I just had a long talk with Mr. Corey Finch of Finch Freight and Transfer," Doc said. "He knows I'm a Pinkerton operative, but he thinks I'm here at the request of his insurance company. I did not disabuse him of that belief."

Raider nodded and took a swallow of the brandy. It wasn't as biting a taste as the whiskey he had just had, but it was better than nothing.

"According to Finch, the freight line has been plagued for the past several months by a series of robberies."

"Yeah?"

"Quite a few of them," Doc said. "Always well planned and well executed and always when there was a load of milled but unrefined gold ore of high value. In short, always when there was a shipment particularly worth the taking. I have been promised the full cooperation of Finch and all his personnel in solving these thefts."

"Thefts, shit," Raider said. "What's that got to do with the railroad?"

"Not a thing that I can see," Doc admitted. "But the ruse certainly gives me a reason to become more familiar with the freight line's operations and people."

"All right," Raider admitted with a grunt. "Reckon I can buy that."

"Now what about you?"

Raider shrugged. "Not much, really. I talked to a few boys around town, at a café an' at a saloon. Didn't want to call attention to myself by being too nosy, but I brought the railroad up. Near as I can see it right now, they all think it would be a good thing if the rails made it. Be good for profits. But they don't think it'll happen."

"Because of the sabotage?"

"No," Raider said. "None of 'em so much as mentioned that. Fact is, if I had to guess I'd say they don't even know nothing about it. No, what they say is that they don't think you can get rails up here t' begin with, an' if you could they don't think they could be kept open for the winter. No matter how much money a fella could spend on the job. They just don't much believe it'll happen. What did Finch say about the railroad?"

"I haven't brought the subject up with him. I thought it best to wait and see if he would mention it himself. So far he hasn't chosen to do so."

"Interesting," Raider said. "A railroad buildin' in this direction, but nobody in Tincup seems to be excited about it worth a damn."

Doc nodded. "They all seem to be legitimately interested in other problems, don't they?"

"Welles ain't."

"True," Doc agreed. He rescued his flask from Raider's grasp, capped it, and put it in his pocket. If he allowed Raider to go unchecked there would be nothing left for Doc's customary nightcap. Doc sighed. "And our job has to do with Mr. Welles and his railroad."

"The sonuvabitch could be right," Raider said. "Finch could be our man. After all, he's the only one I can see as has anything to lose by the railroad gettin' here. The district sure don't. If—an' it's a long if, I got to agree—Welles can get his road operating up here, the district would only gain by it. Except for Finch."

"You don't know the man," Doc said.

Raider thought he could hear something in Weatherbee's voice that implied a certain amount of disbelief in Rutherford Welles' insistence that this Finch fellow was the man behind the sabotage. He gave his partner a hard look.

"Neither do you," Raider said.

Doc did not reply. After a moment Raider stood and headed for the door. It was time he went to his own room. They were not accomplishing a hell of a lot with this conversation.

"What room are you in?" Doc asked. "In case I need to reach you."

"Twenty-one," Raider said.

"All right. Let me know if you learn anything."

"You do the same, Doc. You do the same, hear?" Raider let himself out, checking first to make sure there was no one in the hall to see him leaving the room of a man he was not supposed to know. He headed for No. 21.

CHAPTER TWELVE

"D'you hear there was some more o' them Chinamen killed last night?"

"You don't say."

"Uhuh. One or two, the way I heard it."

Raider kept his attention on the plate in front of him, but his ears remained tuned to the conversation across the table where two men were having their breakfasts too at the common table. He had nothing against a little eavesdropping when the talk might be interesting.

"What happened this time?" the second man asked.

The first shrugged. "Don't know for sure, but I run into a fella earlier that talked to a man who came up over the pass last night. Said he thought these Chinaboys had made them a camp below some rock that somebody blew an' got themsleves made into yella hash when the rock come down on them. He said the railroad boss is mad as shit."

"About a couple Chinamen?" the second man asked incredulously.

"Hell, no. 'Bout havin' to build trestle now when they thought they could just lay track. This man I talked to said the blast wiped out a hundert feet of bed that was all ready for the ties to be laid."

The second man shook his head. "Personally I don't never expect to see tracks reach this town anyhow."

"Me neither," the first said. Their talk shifted to things of greater concern, one arguing that the sensible thing to do would be to start looking for a buyer for their claims so they could get down out of the mountains before winter set in, the other arguing just as strongly that they could make it through another winter and that the quality of their ore might well improve as they went deeper.

"They say Billy Tuttle is laying in five extry wagonloads of whiskey for the winter," one of them said, "an' bringin' in four fresh whores too."

"I don't know," the other said. "Maybe we oughta stay."

Raider put them out of his thoughts and went back to his breakfast.

He wondered if the information had been accurate, if there really had been another sabotage incident during the night. It was possible. But then it was equally possible that these men had only now heard about something that could have happened days or even weeks ago. Or something rumored that had never happened at all. It was impossible to judge.

On the other hand, the local law should be able to tell him if anything had been reported.

Raider didn't want to announce himself as another Pinkerton operative in the neighborhood. But there were ways around that, too. He finished his meal quickly, paid, and left the café.

He stopped first at the nearer of Tincup's two barbershops. Aside from the fact that he genuinely did need a shave, there are few better sources of information than a barber.

This man knew nothing about any sabotage of the rail lines beyond the old incidents Raider had already heard about. He did, however, give a good shave.

"Where's the sheriff's office hereabouts?" Raider asked as he was leaving the man's chair.

"New in town, eh?"

"Yes, why?"

The barber chuckled. "Because it don't take most too long to figure out that we mostly have to make do for ourselves up here."

"There's no local law?"

"Oh, there's a sheriff, all right. But he's way the hell and gone down to Gunnison. Half the year he couldn't get up here if he wanted to. The other half, he don't want to." The barber laughed.

"What do you do for law, then?"

"We got a miner's court, o' course. Legal enough for what we need to handle. An' a couple boys have been deputized in case there's anything serious."

"You don't consider it serious when those Chinese fellows are killed?" Raider asked.

"I didn't say that, now did I?"

"What do you mean, then?"

The barber motioned him to the shop's front window and pointed to the east. "See that tall, bald ridge up there?"

Raider nodded. He remembered it. The road on this side of Tincup Pass ran between the mirrorlike lake and that bare, windswept jumble of rock. When he passed beneath it Raider had been able to see white specks moving across the rocks, mountain goats feeding up there above timberline.

"That ridge line is the dividing point between the counties," the barber said. "Anything that's happened to them Chinese has been on the other side of it. Out of the jurisdiction of our deputies."

"How would I find one of your, uh, deputies, if I wanted to talk to one?"

"They ain't full-time deputies, you understand. There's a couple of them, though. They work for Finch Freight and Transfer." The barber grinned. "That's the sheriff's way of getting out o' coming up here when he can. You might not of heard, but there's been a lot of robberies of the wagons hauling gold down. Finch wagons. So the sheriff went an' deputized some of the freighters so's they could handle the robbery business official."

"I see," Raider said.

Looked at one way it was a logical enough thing to do with distances so far and the frequency of having the few roads snow-filled and impassable.

On the other hand, if Welles was correct and Finch really was behind the railroad sabotage—which as far as Raider could see was still the only logical possibility here—then having Finch people as the local law would be another definite advantage for Corey Finch.

Doc Weatherbee had not come right out and said last night that he believed Finch innocent of Rutherford Welles' accusations. But his attitude had certainly implied it. Raider knew Weatherbee well enough to be able to read that clear as rainwater.

So Raider was going to have to be careful, have to make very sure that his own opinions were not influenced the way Doc's may have been.

Raider scratched his freshly shaven chin and brushed idly at the full, neatly trimmed sweep of his black mustache. Doc was going to have to remember something here: just because T. Rutherford Welles was a prick and an asshole— and the man was guilty on both counts—it did not necessarily follow that he was *wrong*.

It wasn't like Weatherbee to let personal opinions cloud his judgment. But there could be a first time for everything. Raider was going to have to watch out for the both of them on that score, it appeared.

He thanked the barber and paid the man for his services,

then ambled off toward the Finch outfit. He wanted to get a look at some of these deputies and maybe learn a little more about what may or may not have taken place on the railroad right-of-way last night.

CHAPTER THIRTEEN

"You have an admirable operation here," Doc Weatherbee said to Corey Finch. He meant it. He had spent the morning going over Finch's records and reports. Finch was under the impression that Doc's interest had to do with the robberies that had been plaguing the freight company. In truth the entire charade had been leading up to this conversation now that they were taking a break for lunch.

"Thank you," Finch said. "We work at it."

"Obvious," Doc said. "Have you—excuse me, this has nothing to do with the robberies, of course, but I can't help wondering—have you made plans for cutting back once the railroad crosses Tincup Pass and the mines can ship at lower tariffs?"

"None whatsoever," Finch said with a laugh.

Doc raised an eyebrow.

"I know that must sound like a lack of foresight, Weatherbee," the businessman went on, "but really, we have nothing to worry about."

"Why is that? I understood—"

"Oh, there is some construction under way across the pass. I am aware of that. But I have no faith whatever in their ability to reach Tincup." Finch shook his head. "It simply will not happen. I don't worry about them at all."

The man certainly did not *sound* worried in the slightest. Doc had to wonder if such a degree of confidence was based on some form of intimate knowledge that Doc did not possess. Perhaps some knowledge that Corey Finch *should* not possess.

"The sabotage?" Doc asked.

"What?"

"I was wondering if you are so sure about it because of the way someone has been sabotaging the railroad's construction work."

"Of course not. Oh, we hear stories about that sort of thing, but frankly I put little credence in them. I suspect they are no more than the groundwork being laid, excuses in advance of failure, Weatherbee. After all, man, you've been over that pass. Do you believe anyone can drive a railroad over it?"

Doc shrugged.

"Well, I for one do not, sir." Finch stood and reached for his coat. "Shall we go to lunch now?"

"Of course." Doc joined him.

Finch stopped in the office to tell a clerk to have several of the employees report to the office and remain there as soon as they arrived, then they went out into the sunshine for the first time in hours. As they were leaving they passed a bent and wizened little man carrying a mop and pail.

"So early, George?" Finch asked.

"Mr. Satterly, sir. He spilt his inkwell again. They ast me to come get up what of it I could." The little swamper called George chuckled and touched his cap.

"Then remind Alf to pay you for the extra time, George," Finch said.

George touched the brim of his cap, and Finch and Weatherbee walked off toward the Finch house.

"You treat your employees well," Doc observed.

"I certainly try to," Finch said. He smiled. "In old George's case I feel a certain amount of guilt, I think."

"How is that?"

Finch shrugged. "The vagaries of fortune, or something like that. I used to drink heavily myself. Before I met my wife. She is the real reason I've become a success. If it hadn't been for her, why, I could be as bad off as poor George is now. So I have him come in in the evenings and work a few hours tidying up. No one else will hire the poor man. He's not usually reliable, although I must say he seems appreciative of the little I have been able to do for him. He rarely fails to report for work anymore. I think that is a good sign, don't you agree?"

"Could be," Doc said politely. He tried to remember where he had seen George before. After a moment he gave it up. Probably he had noticed the man on the street or in an alley last night.

A man on horseback passed them. A tall, well-set-up man with a revolver on his belt riding a roan horse. Doc knew good and well where he had seen that man before. But he did not acknowledge Raider as he passed.

CHAPTER FOURTEEN

There was no work being done on the shattered roadbed when Raider got there. Instead the crews of Chinese were laboring a hundred feet or more lower on the steep mountainside, using the strength of human muscles to try to clear what must have been hundreds of tons of fallen rock.

Above them, where Raider and his roan were, there was a gap of approximately seventy feet in the ledge where the road was to be built. On both sides of the break was a level bed of crushed and packed rock, ready for ties and rails to be laid.

At least some of the rumor in Tincup had been accurate. Now a trestle would have to be constructed in order to span the section that had been blown out by explosives.

Raider left his horse on the roadbed and climbed carefully down to where the Chinese were working. He had to move slowly and with caution, because a misstep here would have sent him sliding and falling for hundreds of feet.

The white man who was in charge of the workers saw Raider and approached him without welcome. Raider introduced himself.

"Oh," the foreman said. "I heard you were in the area. I'm Tim Crider."

They shook, and Raider tipped his black Stetson back on his head. "Looks like you have the whole bunch busy on this job," he said.

There were so many Chinese involved in the effort, they were getting in each other's way. Cutting the work force in half would really have been more efficient, quite apart from the fact that the remaining men could have been used to the railroad's advantage back up on the bed, working to extend that higher onto the mountain.

"Yeah," Crider said, "and I bet I know what you're thinking, too. What you don't know, though, is that I couldn't get a one of them to do shit up there until this job is taken care of. They'll all be having fits until the bodies are out and packed in brine ready to ship."

"What the hell are you talking about?"

"Got to get the bodies, man. Pickle them and ship 'em back to China. That's part of the deal, y' see. Any of them that dies over here, their bodies get shipped home. A lot of bosses didn't pay much mind to that, but it's the thing that's kept Welles in Chinamen all these years. He might shit on them in lots of ways, but never that one. It's been his ace in the hole all this time."

"Sure would slow things down, though, I'd think."

Crider looked up the mountainside toward the broken ledge where yesterday a railroad bed had run. "Sometimes it doesn't hardly seem like a day doing this will make a lick of difference. If you know what I mean." He sighed. "Now we have to as good as start over with this section. It was all ready till this happened. Now . . . three weeks, maybe a month to cut timbers and span that gap."

"So long? It doesn't look like *that* much of a job."

Crider grunted. "The son of a bitch that set those charges knew what he was doing. A hundred feet in either direction and I could've had the gap closed in a week. But right there where they done it, well, the anchor points are crappy. To get a solid set on the verticals I got to come downslope another five feet. Which means the whole damn bed has to be regraded above and below. I won't know till the surveyors get here and an engineer checks over what I can plainly see, but I'm just hoping we won't have to change the whole stinking section grade just to make up for that five feet. We're running close to the limit as it is, though. It could be touchy."

"Could you show me where the charges were placed?"

Crider looked at him like he was some kind of idiot.

"No, I mean *exactly* where."

"I expect I could."

Crider led the way up the loose footing, puffing and panting from exertion as he did so. The crew boss was not in particularly good condition. But then, at this altitude even Raider was having to slow down and was conscious of the shortness of oxygen.

"Here," he said finally.

Raider could easily see the narrow, half-round depressions in the rock where blasting holes had been drilled. The mountainside remained stable and solid behind them, but the front halves of the drill holes and everything that had been beyond them had been sheared away by the explosions.

"That's what I was wondering," Raider said.

"What's that?"

"If they had found someplace where you could just pack some dynamite against the ground and cause a break like this or if they'd had to drill."

"Huh," Crider said. "I can't think of *any*place where you could just lay some charges down and expect them to do much good. I mean, people as don't know much about explosives, they have a lot of wild ideas about what you can do with powder or dynamite, but most of what they think they know is a lot of shit. To break a ledge off a damn mountain you got to drill and pack and know what you're doing."

"That's kind of what I thought," Raider said. "How long would it take someone—or a crew of several, I'd guess—to prepare to blow the ledge here?"

Crider removed his hat and ran the palm of one hand over a balding scalp. "I hadn't thought about that, but I see what you're getting at." He went back down the mountainside a few yards and looked left and right, assessing with knowledge much greater than Raider's the number and depth of the holes that had had to be drilled in order to slice the rock ledge away from the mountain.

"If there was one drilling crew, with a doublejack, say, they'd have been working three nights at least. Less time, of course, if they had more men who knew what they were doing. The ledge was blown a little after dark last night. We heard the shots, far away as we were."

"Far away?" Raider asked.

"A half mile, maybe more," Crider said. "We moved the camp last week. The location before, we were right down there." He pointed. "Nobody could've drilled while we were all down there without the sound of the hammering being heard."

"If the camp was so far from here, why were those Chinese down below the slide when the ledge fell?"

Crider shrugged. "They likely found something they were trying to scratch for. Likely saw something before we moved the camp and then came back on their own time to get more. Could have been anything. These Chinks will spend hours looking for a piece of turquoise they can sell for a penny. It's like they don't care about time or rate of return; if they can get something for nothing, they'll do anything to get it." He grimaced. "You should've seen them up in Wyoming when we were working on a line up there. Found themselves a little jade, and the whole stinking bunch of them went nuts. They have a thing about jade, no matter how shitty the stuff is."

"You don't care much for your men, do you, Crider?"

"I got to admit that they'll work. The little monkeys sure will work for you."

The man had not answered the question—not directly, anyhow—but Raider let it pass. He began to climb up toward the roadbed, his eyes probing the shattered ground for anything that the drillers might have left behind—a cigar butt, a cigarette stub, anything.

There were no tracks for him to follow. But he had not expected any. Nearly the entire mountainside was made of broken rock. The biggest difference between the side of the mountain and the prepared roadbed was only in the size of the rock and the fact that the roadbed had been compacted. A horseshoe might cause a scrape but not a track on either surface. A man's boots would leave no mark whatsoever. After a while Raider gave up. He could find nothing. If the drillers had left anything behind, the clues would all have been swept away with the fall of the ledge.

"You're sure there were men down there when the ledge came down?" Raider asked.

"My straw boss said there was. That's good enough for me," Crider told him.

"Your straw boss?"

"One of the Chinks. He speaks pretty good English. Want to talk to him?"

Raider shook his head. He did not need to talk with the Chinese. Nor did he particularly want to see the bodies when they were eventually uncovered. If, that is, there was enough left of the men to identify as having once been something human. Bodies he had seen a bellyful of already, thank you.

Besides, he wanted to get back to Tincup. That miner at breakfast had already heard about the incident. From a traveler who had come up during the night, the man had said.

The idea of anyone traveling Tincup Pass at night sounded unlikely at best. So it was at least possible that the miner had heard the story from one of the men who was trying to stop the progress of the railroad. From him directly or from someone who had unknowingly talked to one of the men Raider was interested in.

The next question was going to be how Raider could locate one of the men who had sat across from him at breakfast this morning.

He returned to the roan and headed back up the mountain, more than half convinced, the more he thought about it, that whoever was trying to destroy T. Rutherford Welles' railroad was headquartered in Tincup. Which, of course, was where Finch Freight and Transfer happened to be headquartered.

CHAPTER FIFTEEN

A player piano was off in one corner, rattling its own keys in a loud, gay tune. Near it men were clustered around a faro table and a roulette outfit. The bar was crowded, the customers noisy. Raider bought himself a beer and moved down to the free lunch counter. He reached for a pickled egg, then thought about what Crider said about pickling the bodies of the dead Chinese and instead took some sliced beef and a handful of crackers.

There was no room at the bar for him to stand, so he carried his mug and small plate of food to a vacant table. Raider sat with his back to the side wall and looked around the crowded saloon, trying to spot either of the men who had been across the table from him this morning. Neither seemed to be there. But then the town had a fair number of other saloons where they might be instead. It was even remotely possible, of course, that neither of them would be out on the town this evening, although judging from the way men were continuing to crowd into the saloons along the street, that possibility seemed slim.

Raider waited there for a little while, then moved on to another place, bought another beer. This time he left the free lunch counter alone. It was not that he was no longer hungry. Knowing he would be spending the evening drinking, he intended to have his supper for free. But the display of assorted cold cuts and crackers in this place looked like they were the original items stocked when the place first opened for business. And that had been quite some time ago.

A dark-haired whore who could never have hoped to make a living in any town larger or more accessible than Tincup tried to get Raider to buy her a drink. He refused.

"Bastard," she mumbled.

"Not that I know of," Raider said agreeably, refusing to let the homely woman ruffle him.

The whore sniffed loudly and turned away, draping herself over the shoulder of a drunk at a nearby table. The drunk groped happily under her short skirt, and the woman leaned down to whisper something to him. He nodded, and they left together, heading for a hallway leading into the back of the building.

Taste, Raider reflected. The wonders of it never ceased to amaze him. He raised his glass in a silent salute to the departing happy couple.

He had not yet seen any female in the town that he would care to bed. Not one that was remotely acceptable.

Raider grinned to himself and amended the thought. None that he was hard up enough to want *yet*.

"Want to share the joke, luv?" a female voice asked from somewhere near his right ear.

Raider turned to look at her. He blinked and looked again.

Things were improving in Tincup, by damn.

The girl was younger than any of the others he had seen here. And she damn sure was better-looking.

She wouldn't win any prizes for sheer beauty, he admitted, but she was a sight better than anything else around.

She was probably in her twenties still, and contrived to make herself look even younger. She had a full figure and hair the color of dark honey.

Probably the only thing that kept her out of the better places in the better towns was a scar that started beneath her right eye and continued raggedly onto her nose. Another scar began just over the eye and ran up into her hairline. She must have taken a hell of a pounding at some time in the past.

"Hello," Raider said. He used the toe of his boot to hook a leg of the chair beside him and shove it away from the table in an invitation for her to sit.

"Thank you." She sat and leaned forward, allowing her blouse to gap open so he could get a better look at the melons she carried there. "Buy me a drink, honey?"

"Sure, why not."

"It'll only be tea. But I suppose you know that." She smiled—he thought she had a rather pretty smile—and put a hand on his knee.

"I know," he said.

"Good." She turned and motioned to someone behind the bar. When the tea came, Raider paid a whiskey price for it. He did not feel cheated. The girl had been honest about it.

She sipped delicately at her shot glass of tea, and Raider felt a perfectly natural response as her hand roved north from his knee and stroked the inside of his thigh.

"I, uh—"

"Janie," a voice interrupted. "C'mere, you little bitch you."

A very tall, blockily built man had taken up a position on the other side of the girl. He took her roughly by the shoulder and pulled at her, nearly spilling her out of the chair.

Raider stood.

The man, whoever he was, was not wearing a gun. The observation was annoying to Raider.

The man's temper was apparently as close to the surface as Raider's. He glared at Rade with a snarl and said, "You open your face, asshole, and I'll break it for you. I just got in from a rough haul, and I'm fixing to have me some fun. So don't you get in my way, or I'll step on you."

Raider grinned at him. "Mister," he said, "you just found all the outlet you're gonna be able to handle for the next few days, so if you need to blow off some steam, why, have at it."

The man's response was a slashing, backhanded left. He did not take the time to turn or to set himself, he just let it fly. Any man who was unprepared for that sudden assault— and most would have been completely unprepared—would have had their heads handed to them without a second blow ever being thrown.

Raider was not so easily taken. He leaned back and let the man's fist whistle harmlessly past, then quickly raised a forearm to block aside the right that followed as the man spun and tried again.

Rade stepped forward and delivered a rapid combination of lefts and rights to the bigger man's gut. Raider was still grinning.

The man backed away. He looked slightly puzzled. He set himself with his arms up and hands fisted, then moved forward again.

Raider let the fellow take his shot, an overhand right that started from way back and looped forward toward Raider's head—

Except Raider's head was no longer in that spot. He darted to his left, moving forward as he did so, and pummeled the man's right kidney with quick, hard punches that would likely leave the fellow pissing blood for the next day or two.

The man howled and turned.

Raider was already moving again, to his right this time, so that the whirling man turned too far. This time Raider jolted his other kidney.

"You don't fight fair, you sonuvabitch," the big man wailed.

"You got that right, buddy," Raider agreed. He stepped back and let the fellow come to him.

The man jabbed awkwardly with his left. Raider ignored it, waiting for the hard right that was sure to follow. It did, as expected, and Raider blocked it with his left forearm and followed with a hard, straight right of his own that landed on the bridge of the man's nose. Flesh split open, and blood began to flow freely into the man's drooping mustache.

The big fellow blinked and backed off.

"Come again, friend. Anytime," Raider invited.

The fellow pulled a filthy bandanna from his hip pocket and tried without much success to staunch the flow of blood that continued to pour from his damaged nose.

"You got big troubles, bud," the big man warned darkly. "My pal's a deppity sherf here. He's gonna throw you in the jug for this."

"Sure he is," Raider agreed.

The big man turned and lumbered away, weaving his way through the crowd and out the front door of the saloon.

The girl—the man had called her Janie—took Raider's elbow. He had almost forgotten about her, even though she was the reason for the scrap.

She looked worried.

"Sit down," Raider said. "Finish your drink."

She shuddered. "You don't know him. He'll do it. He really will."

"Bull," Raider said calmly. "The idiot had too much to drink. Soon as he sobers up, he'll know it."

"But until then he might bring back some of his bull-whacker friends. And some of them *are* deputies, mister.

They could put you in jail for the night. And if he's mad at me too..."

Raider shrugged. "So we'll get out of sight. You and me both." He smiled at her. "It's the least I can do for you. And I won't claim that I'm all that unhappy about it."

"He knows where my room is," the still worried Janie said.

"Could be, but he don't know where *mine* is. Come along."

Janie nodded and took Raider's arm. He led her out onto the street and turned toward the hotel where he was staying.

He was not, as he had already admitted to her, unhappy about the situation.

And hell, with any luck at all, she might be grateful enough to give out discounts this evening.

CHAPTER SIXTEEN

Raider unlocked the hotel room door and held it open for Janie to enter. She seemed surprised by the small courtesy, almost confused by it.

As soon as the door was closed and locked behind them she began removing her clothes. Not until she was naked— her body as fine, and as unblemished, as Raider had hoped— did she hold her hand out in an unspoken request for payment.

"How much?" Raider asked.

"Two dollars?" It was as much a question as an answer. It was perfectly obvious from her tone of voice that if he objected she would accept less. The going rate in Tincup, he suspected, should be more like a single dollar for the services of one of the ordinary whores of the town. On the other hand, Janie was decidedly superior to any of the others he had seen. She probably would have been able to command nearly any price she chose to set. Yet she did not seem aware of her advantage.

Raider gave her the amount she requested, offering no argument about it. She accepted the money from him and turned to place it with the clothing she had folded carefully and laid on the one chair in the small room.

When she turned her back to him he could see that her body was not at all unblemished.

Her back, which should have been sleek and lovely, was marred with an ugly mass of crisscrossed welts.

They were not old scars, either. They were still red, still quite fresh. They were painful merely to look at and must have been an agony to bear, yet she did not mention them, to pretend they did not exist.

Raider walked up behind her. She tried to turn to face him, but he stopped her with a hand on her shoulder.

Janie stiffened under his touch.

Gently Raider laid a fingertip lightly on the raised swelling of one of the lesser welts. Even at that slight contact she winced and bit her underlip.

"A customer?" he asked.

She bit her lip again, hesitated, then nodded.

"Look at me," he said.

She turned. For a brief moment her eyes met his, then dropped away to stare fixedly at the buttons of his shirt.

"Not a customer," he said. It was no question.

"It doesn't matter," she said. Abruptly she raised her chin so she could look at him. A false, professional smile twisted her lips. "C'mon, honey. Whatever you want. You'll get your money's worth." She winked at him. "That's a promise from me to you, honey."

Raider looked at her for a moment. "All right," he said softly.

He stepped backward and stood there where he could get a better look at her.

She was a delectable item. Her breasts were full but

reasonably firm, her nipples small and dark. Her stomach was unusually flat above a curly, brown patch of pubic hair. Her waist was very small.

If she had any flaws—any natural ones, that is—it would have been in the slight heaviness of her thighs.

Raider decided he might be able to forgive her that minor imperfection.

She helped him undress, and he took her by the hand and led her to the bed.

"Whatever you want, honey," she said again.

Raider lay down on his back. Normally he would have preferred a simple coupling and release, but if he placed her under him—and he had no doubt that she would do that if he requested it—the contact of cheap sheeting against the wounds on her back would be agonizing. He did not want to put her through that. Better this time to allow her to remain on top.

When he lay like that, his erection pulsing strongly toward the ceiling, Janie misunderstood what he wanted. She knelt beside his waist and bent to take him into her mouth.

After a moment she shifted sideways, still holding him between her lips, and moved so that she was kneeling between his widespread legs. She mouthed him hungrily and used both hands to cup and tease his balls.

"So big," she mumbled once when she withdrew from him a fraction of an inch. The comment was the simple truth—experience had told him that years ago—but he always resented such a remark when it came from a working girl. It always sounded too professional to him to be taken seriously.

He let her work him over that way, enjoying the feel of it, the wet heat and the suction, but it was not the way he wanted to finish. He was in no hurry, though, and she was good at what she was doing.

Well before he felt the rise of pressure in his balls that would signal an approaching climax he reached down to cup her chin in his hand and lift her away.

Janie wrapped her lips around him tighter, sucking on him greedily as he pulled her away. The engorged head of his cock popped free from her mouth with a loud, moist plop.

She looked up at him and winked, then laughed lightly. Raider laughed with her.

He pulled her up until she lay on top of him, her face nuzzling into his neck. Her hands remained behind, trapped between their bodies. She fondled and toyed with him, running her fingers over his balls and his cock continuously while she began to lick his neck.

Her tongue roved down onto his chest. She rolled her head from side to side, licking at one nipple and then at the other and then back up to his neck. Raider sighed and shifted in comfortable contentment on the bed.

Janie seemed in no hurry to finish him, and he did not prompt her to end the pleasures.

After a while her hands left him and pressed lightly against his chest. She raised herself from him slowly, taking her time about it, dragging her heavy breasts over the sensitized flesh of his chest, lightly rubbing her nipples against his.

Damned interesting, he conceded. Damned nice, too.

She changed position again, straddling his waist, and lowered herself so that her sex, moist and gaping wide, was pressed against his belly.

She did something, some kind of contraction of internal muscles he had not even been sure women *had,* and the effect was much like a gentle kiss. But a kiss the likes of which he had never had before.

Raider's eyebrows went up in surprise, and Janie laughed with what sounded like genuine delight.

"You're kidding," he said.

She shook her head and giggled.

"Bet you can't do it again," he challenged.

Her answer was a wink and a grin. She stuck her tongue out at him.

"No you can't," he said.

Janie moved up again to straddle his chest. Bracing herself with the tips of her fingers on his shoulders, she lowered herself until that other set of wet lips was poised over his right nipple.

She settled lower until her flesh was just barely in contact with his.

And did it again.

The muscles inside her contracted sharply. This time he could see the effort of it clench the flat plane of her belly.

He laughed aloud.

The effect was *very* much like a kiss.

But damned well different, too.

Janie laughed with him. Then moved to the other side and "kissed" him that way again.

Still laughing, Raider reached up to cup her breasts in his hands. They were full and soft, warm and yielding. He squeezed lightly, running his thumbnails over her nipples. Janie tossed her head back and closed her eyes.

After a moment she pulled away from him and backed down his body until his throbbing cock was bumping against the crack of her round ass. She raised herself and, without once having to use her hands to guide him, trapped him within her wide, wet lips.

She lowered her body over his, skewering herself on his shaft and taking him deep into herself.

Raider moaned.

She put her hands, fingers spread wide, onto his chest and began to pump slowly up and down, in and out.

She shifted position again, getting off her knees so that she was squatting with one foot on either side of his waist. When she had done that, without ever losing contact with him, she was able to move faster, to stroke harder and deeper.

Raider felt the heat, the sucking pull of her wet flesh on his. He felt the rise of pressure, the growing sensations of pleasure.

Once, then again, she paused when she had him held fully within her. She stopped for a moment and contacted those hidden muscles. He could see the power of it flex under the deceptively soft skin of her belly.

The grip of her around the shaft of his cock felt as strong as the clenching of a fist, introducing a new sensation to the act and heightening the feeling for him.

With a warm smile of apparently genuine pleasure, Janie went back to stroking him.

He was ready now. He tried to lie still beneath her as he had been throughout, but now the growing pressure was too much to permit that.

Raider's hips began to respond involuntarily to Janie's demanding touch.

His back arched violently upward, and with a groan of satisfaction he spewed wetly inside her, the hot flow pouring into a space already filled to capacity and then flooding out again, hot and sticky, over his balls.

"Ahhhh!"

Janie sat down hard against him, pressing her weight against his pelvic bones, prolonging the climax for him.

When he was done, when the last possible droplet had been wrung from him, she raised herself, allowing him to drop free, his flagging erection subsiding onto the sticky, matted bed of soaked hair at his crotch.

She chuckled and bent to him, using her mouth and her tongue to cleanse him of his own fluids and of any that she might have left behind.

The girl knew what she was doing, Raider thought. She damn sure did.

Without thinking, without realizing, Raider petted her, his hand running lightly over the back of her head and down across her shoulders to her back.

Janie winced. The pain of the contact with her whip-torn flesh was too great. She cried out.

For a moment Raider felt like a son of a bitch. He had forgotten. He would not deliberately have caused the girl pain, not for anything.

But someone had.

Janie had been good to him. Two dollars was not enough of a price for the girl to have gone out of her way to give him such pleasure.

But some son of a prick had gone greatly out of his way to give this girl intense and lasting pain.

Raider wondered just who that bastard might be.

CHAPTER SEVENTEEN

Doc Weatherbee was comfortable. And he was finding that fact to be alarming.

Once again he was a guest in the home of Mr. and Mrs. Corey Finch, and he was extremely comfortable there. The Finches were a pleasure to be with, their home and their company a pleasure to share.

Doc knew damned good and well that the pleasure he was taking with them threatened his objectivity on this assignment. He was already having to admit to himself that he did not *want* Rutherford Welles' accusations to be true. He did not *want* to learn that Corey Finch might be in any way involved with the sabotage of Welles' railroad.

And that knowledge distressed him.

He was caught, trapped on a double-edged hook. If Doc persisted in his efforts to investigate Corey Finch, he would necessarily feel guilty about the deception of a host who could well have been, who could well still *become,* a good friend. Yet if he did *not,* Doc would not be fulfilling his obligations to the Pinkerton Agency.

He had to content himself with the thought that he would be doing both Finch and the Pinkerton Agency a service by *dis*proving Welles' accusations. If that were possible. Be cause Finch remained the only logical suspect in the sabotage of the railroad.

Yet, damn it, Doc did not *want* to believe Finch guilty of such a crime. He liked Finch. He enjoyed his company. He enjoyed now the pleasant evening before a fire in the Finch parlor with Corey sharing brandy and cigars and a well-contested chess match while Mrs. Finch sat nearby, half-glasses perched on the bridge of her nose while she quietly tatted a lace something-or-other that was still too small to be recognizable.

Doc sighed with a mixture of pleasure and unhappiness and leaned forward to move his bishop three spaces and bring Finch's knight under attack.

Corey Finch smiled and reached toward a rook.

His hand never reached the piece. The game was interrupted by a loud knocking at the front door. The power and the speed of the rapping conveyed an urgency that had not been in the room until that moment.

"I'll get it," Finch said. He left the board and hurried to the door.

"Corey. Quick," an out-of-breath male voice reached the parlor. "Tom Prate's recognized one of the robbers. They got 'im cornered on the top floor of Sada's place."

Doc leaped to his feet and joined Finch at the open doorway, the chess game forgotten.

Finch grabbed his hat and a heavy jacket from the wall hooks beside the door.

"I'm coming with you," Doc said.

"Good."

Both men left the house at a run, quickly passing the already winded man who had brought the message. Doc had no idea where this Sada's place was. He followed Finch.

Sada's place turned out to be a whorehouse on a quiet back street of Tincup. It was one of the few two-story buildings in the town.

A group of hard-faced freighters were ranked around the outside of the building. More of Finch's men stood in the open doorway, waiting for their boss.

"Are you sure about him, Tom?" Finch asked.

A short, cocky-looking man wearing lace-up boots and a plaid mackinaw turned. He nodded. "Damn right I'm sure, Corey. He's one of 'em, all right. Three weeks ago when they hit my rig for twelve thousand from the Cumberland Company, the son of a bitch's mask slipped down. I got a good look at him then an' swore I wouldn't forget that face. Well, tonight I seen him. He went upstairs with that little half-breed girl they call Junebug. I got a real good look at him."

"Does he know you're onto him?"

By way of answer, the freighter pointed toward a Finch man standing nearby. The man was holding his left arm at an awkward angle, and fresh blood dripped from his fingertips onto the rug at the entrance to Sada's. "He winged Eddie when we tried to rush him up the stairs. I kinda think he knows," the freighter said.

Finch frowned. "If we had some regular law up here . . ." His voice died away. After a moment he turned to Doc and explained, "This gang knows that the only deputies up here are my people. The county sheriff deputized some of my people rather than pay to keep a full-time deputy in the mountains. And I'm afraid they must know that my boys will have little sympathy or kindness for them if any are caught. We do not enjoy being robbed and held at gunpoint, you understand."

"I could try to talk him out," Doc said. "He might surrender to a Pinkerton operative. If he's been around at all, he must know that we're square."

Finch paused for a moment to think it over. He nodded. "If you're willing to try it, Doc."

"Of course. Where is he?" Doc asked of the freighter.

The man pointed. "Right up to the top o' them stairs, mister. But be damn careful. He'll likely try an' blow your head off if he gets a look at you first."

Doc looked around. The hallway where they now stood held only Finch men with revolvers and even a few rifles held at the ready. A cluster of handsomely dressed whores and their much older madam were huddled in a corner of the parlor off to the right. Doc beckoned for the madam to come, which she did reluctantly.

"How many of your girls are upstairs?" Doc asked.

She looked into the sitting room, then glanced nervously up the stairwell and back into the sitting room. "Just two," she said. "One of them is my best girl. You'll save her, won't you, mister? The redhead. You will save her, won't you?"

Doc got the impression, uncharitable though it might have been, that it would be acceptable if the lesser girl had to be sacrificed but not the top money-maker. "If I can," he said.

The madam scurried back to the safety of the parlor, and Doc turned to Finch. "Have your boys hold their fire, Corey. And it wouldn't hurt if you gave the order loud enough for our friend upstairs to hear."

Finch shouted his instructions. His voice boomed through the foyer and could not have been missed by the desperate gang member at the top of the stairs.

Doc waited a moment until there was silence. Then he approached the foot of the stairs and went partway up.

"You up there. Can you hear me?"

"What the fuck d'you want?"

"I assume you can hear me, then. Good. My name is Weatherbee. I am an operative of the Pinkerton Detective Agency."

"So?"

"So you can give yourself up to me. I can guarantee you fair treatment and a trail. Not here. I can take you to Gunnison for trial by a competent court of law. There will be no summary judgments. I can promise you that."

"How do I know you're telling the truth?"

"Let the women come down unharmed. I'm willing to accept that as your guarantee. If you do that, I will come up and show you my identification. I'm not armed. Will you do that? We don't want bloodshed here. Including yours. There doesn't have to be any more shooting."

"I don't believe you, man."

"I understand that. If you send the ladies down unhurt, though, I will be willing to believe you. I'll come up unarmed and with my hands in full view at all times. We can talk. You won't be hurt. I promise you that."

"You just want to get me where you can put a bullet in my back."

"Bull," Doc said. "If you've been in the business any time at all you know about the Pinkertons. You know you don't want us after you, but you know too that we'll be straight with you. If we say it, we'll do it."

"I've heard that," the man said grudgingly.

Doc edged a few steps further up the staircase. Then another. He could see over the landing to the second-floor hallway.

The gunman had two whores, one of them with red hair and the other a blonde, and a naked, petrified customer standing in front of him. He was backed up against the far end of the hall. The revolver in his hand was nudging the right ear of the red-haired girl.

"Give me a chance," Doc pleaded. "It's the only way you can possibly get out of here alive. And I know you don't want anyone else to be hurt. You're only suspected of robbery, you know. That isn't a hanging offense. If you give yourself up I'll make sure the judge knows that. I can't make you any promises, but it might help lighten your sentence. I won't try to tell you that you won't have to do

time. We both know better than that. But you won't hang.
You will live to be a free man again." Doc inched up another
step and raised his hands with both empty palms facing the
frightened gunman. "Let the girls and the gentleman come
down. I'll stay right here. You can watch me at all times.
You can use me as your hostage instead of them."

There was a sound of something falling downstairs, a
crash of shattered glass. The gunman jumped, the muzzle
of his gun jabbing into the side of the redheaded whore's
ear. The girl—she was quite pretty—began to cry.

"Aw, shit," the gunman said.

"Let them go," Doc said. He moved up another step,
exposing his chest to the gunman. He really was unarmed.
His .38 Colt was back in his hotel room inside his bag. "We
can work this out."

"I don't know, man."

"You don't want any of these people to be hurt," Doc
said. 'You aren't a killer. You don't want to die, and you
don't want them to die." He went up one more step.

"Shit, man."

"Let them come ahead."

Doc took a chance. He pointed to the blond girl and
motioned her toward him, then the shivering customer who
had been with one or the other of the whores.

The girl hesitated. The man moved first. He glanced back
over his shoulder at the gunman. All four of the people at
the end of the hall were pale. One looked to be as scared
as the next. The robber looked just as frightened as were
his hostages.

The customer gave his captor a worried look, then with
a short, squeaking cry of relief bolted forward. The blond
girl and then the redhead hurried quickly behind him.

The three brushed past Doc and ran down the staircase.

"Thank you," Doc said calmly. "I'll make sure the judge
knows you allowed that."

"I don't know . . ." The robber turned the muzzle of his
revolver toward Doc.

The man really did not want to fire. Doc could see that the hammer of the single-action revolver was not cocked.

Doc took another step up and another. He moved up onto the floor of the hallway and stood with his hands spread wide.

"Do you want to see my identification?"

"No, I . . . I seen you before."

"You know that I'm a Pinkerton."

"Yeah, I . . . I do."

"Good." Doc took a step toward him. He continued slowly forward, being very careful not to make any sudden moves. When he was face to face with the man he slowly lowered his left hand, palm up. "Give me your gun now. I'll take you down. Stay right beside me. No one will hurt you."

The man swallowed. He seemed indecisive.

"It will be all right. You don't have to worry."

The man closed his eyes and squeezed them tightly shut. His face crumpled into an expression of despair. His shoulders slumped, the tension of the past minutes leaving him, and he handed Doc the revolver.

"Thank you," Doc said again. He shoved the uncocked weapon into his waistband and put an arm around the gunman's shoulders. "Thank you."

Doc led the man down the stairs. He could feel the trembling of fear in the man's shoulders.

"It's all right," Doc called ahead. "Back your boys off, Corey. Tell them it's all under control now."

He waited until he heard Finch issuing the orders before he continued down the stairs with his prisoner.

When they were on the ground floor Doc took a set of handcuffs form his hip pocket and snapped them onto the wrists of the gunman, who was looking with terror from one unfriendly face to another as Corey Finch's freighters crowded around.

"You fellows can clear out now," Doc told them. "Go home now. This is all over."

When only he and Finch and the prisoner remained in

the foyer, Doc led the robber outside. The night air was cold. It felt invigorating. It also was damned uncomfortable when it reached the sweat that had been flowing from him. Doc had not realized at the time just how nervous he must have been.

They paused on the steps, and Doc turned to Finch. He had no idea where they should be going now. If there was a jail in Tincup he did not know where it was.

He opened his mouth to speak, but before he could, another sound shattered the quiet of the night.

Flame, yellow and blindingly bright, lanced out from somewhere to Doc's left, and the muzzle report of a rifle reverberated among the buildings along the quiet street.

The handcuffed prisoner jerked, and the right side of his head burst outward in an explosion of pink spray.

A bullet had entered his left temple. The exit of the soft slug had turned the whole right side of his head into a red and gray mush.

The lifeless body collapsed onto the ground at Doc's feet.

Men came pouring out of the whorehouse and racing around to the front of the building from all sides, where the freighters had been posted to block any escape attempts.

Every one of them had guns in their hands. Any one of them could have fired the shot.

Doc looked helplessly from face to face, recognizing few of them—Tom Prate, the others who had been inside, freighters and hostlers and even old George, the drunk who cleaned up in the Finch offices.

Doc swore bitterly and stalked away from the scene before he might say something that he would regret afterward. But whoever had fired that shot had made a mockery of Doc Weatherbee's oath, and that he could neither tolerate nor change.

CHAPTER EIGHTEEN

Janie looked nervous. She kept glancing from one side of
the room to the other. Yet at the same time she looked like
she was pleased, almost proud. They were having a late
supper in the hotel dining room—which was a somewhat
optimistic way of putting it; the restaurant was attached to
the hotel but was a scant cut above the quality of the other
greasy-spoon cafés in the town—and the girl seemed to
consider it quite a treat for a man to actually let himself be
seen in polite company with her. Yet at the same time she
looked more than a trifle nervous about the presence on the
other side of the room of several nicely dressed and obviously respectable ladies of the community.

She was making the most of the occasion, and Raider
had allowed her to order both tea and a wine with her meal.
His own tastes were more easily served.

The waiter had hesitated only once about accepting Janie's
order. A hard, cutting flash of Raider's dark eyes had chilled

any disapproval the snotty little prick might have expressed.

When the girl was done and pushed her plate away, Raider offered dessert.

"No, thank you. I couldn't hold another thing." She dabbed at her lips daintily with a napkin and was obviously trying her best to mind her manners in an unfamiliar situation.

"Would you mind telling me something?" Raider asked.

She frowned. "You mean, what's a nice girl like me doing in my line of work?"

Rade laughed. "No, honey. Nothing like that."

She blushed. "Sorry. But I bet you wouldn't believe how many fellas think they can rescue a soiled dove."

"Really?"

"Yeah. It's weird. But I've thought about it a lot. What I think it is, they all o' them want to rescue a workin' girl so they can have themselves a grateful little doxie and spend the rest of their dirty little lives holding it over her and feeling superior to her. You know?"

"Could be," Raider said. "Yeah, it just could be."

"I shoulda known you weren't like that." She reached across the table to lightly touch the back of his wrist. "You really *are* a nice guy, aren't you."

Raider chuckled. "I can't say as I'm real used to that, but I thank you."

"Anyway, honey, anything you wanta ask me, you go right ahead. I'll either tell you the truth or tell you I won't answer at all. No fibs. Okay?"

Raider patted her hand and said, "What it is, I'd like to meet the fellow who, uh, runs the girls in town."

Genuine pleasure leapt into Janie's eyes. "Oh, wow. Are you in the business, honey? I'd love to work for you. I really would. An' gosh, honey, I'd do anything for you. There wouldn't be any end to the tricks I could turn for you. The money'd be *real* good. I promise you. An' I wouldn't *never* hold back on you. Not a penny. I could make a bunch of money for a swell man like you. I just know I could."

Raider smiled at her. He made no attempt to dissuade her from the idea that he was a whoremaster in search of a stable. "Then you'll take me to the man, Janie?"

"Oh, sure, honey. That'd be great."

"Good." Raider paid for their meal, being damn well careful to not leave a penny of tip for the smart-ass waiter, and Janie led the way outside and into the residential section of Tincup.

"How is this working here?" he asked as they walked.

"The guy that runs us is—well, I better not mention his name, 'cause his wife an' the church an' everything would just shit if they knew what he does—but anyway, he has the control, see. What he does is rent us out to whoever wants some girls in his joint. He has a couple regular houses too for the fancy trade." She sighed. "I'd be in a nice place like that too except I opened my big mouth one time when I oughtn't to, and I got this." She touched the scars on the side of her face.

"It sounds like you have a discipline problem, Janie."

"Oh, not with you. Never. I can *promise* you that. I wouldn't *never* give you no trouble. But, yeah." She shuddered. "Me and him, we don't get along so good."

"He's the one put the cat on your back?"

"Yeah," she admitted. "I didn't think I deserved it. Honest I didn't. But then what the hell do *I* know. He tore me up some anyhow."

"You say nobody knows about the business he's in?"

"Naw. Nobody. He'd really be pissed if any of us told. So when we get there—gee, I'll have to tell you his name or you won't know who to ask for—anyway, when we get there I'll show you, and then I'd better split. Or you won't have nothing much of value to rent if you're thinking of taking me on."

Raider nodded.

Every few steps Janie would turn and grin at him. Apparently the prospect of having Raider for her new boss pleased her immensely.

"You wouldn't mind if I got you out from under this man completely, would you, Janie?" Raider asked.

Her eyes widened, and her damaged face lit up with joy. "You mean buy me out? All the way out? Gosh, honey, for that I'd do *any*thing. For you I'd do the kind of crap that he makes us do for punishment when he has his nasty pals in."

Raider's eyebrows went up.

"You know," she said matter-of-factly. "Donkeys an' shit like that. Needles. You know." She shuddered again.

"Yeah," Raider said drily. "I know."

They walked on in silence. After a few minutes she stopped and pointed to a largish house with lamplight showing from its curtained windows. There was a low fence built around the front yard. The yard was much more substantial than those around it. The fence was painted a neat and pretty white.

"His name is Wentworth, honey. Bryce Wentworth."

"Thanks." Raider cupped her chin in his large hand and tipped her head back. He leaned down and kissed her at the corner of her eye, on the scar that marred her looks.

She shivered, which might have been from pleasure or might as easily have been from the nip in the air, then turned and ran back toward the business district, where the saloons were still busy and the girls still working.

Raider watched her go, then turned and approached the Wentworth house.

His knock was answered by a matronly woman of imposing girth and truly remarkable ugliness. Raider removed his hat and smiled at the woman. "Is Mr. Wentworth in, ma'am?"

"One moment," she said. She closed the door and left him on the front porch.

A minute later he heard the approach of footsteps, and a man opened the door. The man was in his shirtsleeves and held a newspaper in his hands.

Raider had seen the man before. It took him a second or two to remember where. When he did he almost laughed. Bryce Wentworth was the barber who had shaved him.

"I have some business to discuss with you," Raider said.

Wentworth glanced back inside his house, then into the shadows that lay around them. "I talk business at my shop," he whispered. "Never here."

"I really think you'll want to talk to me tonight, Bryce. I really think you will."

Wentworth, who was a skinny, ineffectual-looking man, licked his lips in indecision and shot another nervous glance inside. "Back in a moment, dear," he called. He fetched a coat from inside the door and went out on the porch.

"Not so close to the windows, I think," Raider said. He walked down into the yard, Wentworth following.

Much of the yard was dark, the lamplight from the house windows failing to reach the limits of the fenced property.

Raider led Wentworth into a far corner of the yard, the smaller man trailing nervously behind. "You shouldn't come here like this," he was saying.

Funny, Raider thought, how a man could be such a terror with defenseless whores yet be so uncomfortable in the presence of a grown man.

But then, Raider thought, maybe one naturally followed the other. Maybe a shit like Wentworth could only feel strong and manly when he was beating up on a woman.

The idea of any son of a bitch who would take a whip to a woman disgusted Raider. Which was something he intended to mention to good old Bryce here.

Raider reached the limits of the yard and turned. Wentworth was a pace or two behind.

As soon as Wentworth was in the exact position Raider wanted, Rade's boot lashed up and forward. He buried the toe of his boot in Wentworth's crotch. The beginnings of a shriek were cut short, and the bastard fainted.

Raider hunkered on the ground beside Wentworth. He pulled a bit of dried weed from the ground and chewed on the stem reflectively and patiently while he waited for Wentworth to come around.

When he did, Raider smiled down at him with false sympathy. "My oh my," Rade said. "Did that hurt?"

"You . . ." Wentworth took a look into the steel in Raider's eyes and wisely shut his mouth.

"Tell me, Bryce, how is it that folks around here think a barber is doing so well?"

"Investments," Wentworth whispered. "I'm into investments."

Raider smiled at him. "Uh huh. And so you are. They just don't know what *kind* of investments."

Wentworth groaned and tried without much success to raise himself into a sitting position. Raider obligingly helped.

"Feel better now?"

Wentworth scowled.

"What I wanted to talk to you about, ol' buddy, is the way you treat your girls."

"They're my fucking girls to—" Wentworth began hotly.

His protests were cut short with a backhanded slap that knocked him flat onto his back again and started a flow of blood from the corners of his mouth.

"Careful how you talk to me, Bryce," Raider said calmly. "I don't think you want to make me mad."

"But—"

Raider's hand flashed out again. Another spill of blood came from the other side of Wentworth's mouth.

"We don't want to be unpleasant with one another, Bryce, now do we?" Raider was smiling. Wentworth was not.

"No," the smaller man said. He struggled up, and again Raider helped him.

"What it is," Raider said, "is that you're getting out of the business, Bryce. All the way out."

"You can't—"

Raider chopped him in the throat. Wentworth rolled over, gagging and gasping for breath. "To tell you the truth, Bryce, I believe that I can." Raider waited until he had the barber's attention again. "Do you disagree?"

Wentworth shook his head.

"That's nice," Rade said. "So here's the way it is. You're quitting the business. You and I both know that those girls aren't going to be able to handle things without someone to direct them. So what you're gonna do is turn them over to the boys that've been renting from you. No charge, of course. You just turn them over, scot-free. From now on, Bryce, you leave them be. I mean, man, you don't even *hire* any of them again. And there won't be any more whips or donkeys or needles or razors or whatever else you might have used on any of the poor bitches. I mean, you're done with that sort of thing. You understand me?"

Wentworth nodded.

"That's right, Bryce. From now on if you want a little ass, you talk to your missus about it. Or her and every other decent person in Tincup is gonna know all about the kind of man Bryce Wentworth *used* to be. And I say 'used' to be, because that's what it will be for you if you *ever* fuck around with one of those girls again. You understand me, Bryce? You understand what I'm telling you?"

For emphasis Raider's Remington revolver appeared in his hand, materializing as if by magic directly beneath Bryce Wentworth's nose. Raider prodded his left nostril with the cold steel and watched a thin sheen of sweat form on Wentworth's brow.

"Now, Bryce, I believe you are beginning to understand me."

"Uh huh," the man croaked.

Raider smiled at him and returned the Remington to his holster.

He stood and helped the barber to his feet, then turned the little man around and brushed off the back of his coat and the seat of his trousers. "There," he said. "Wouldn't do for to walk in the house looking all mussed and fussed up, would it?"

"No," Wentworth said weakly.

"I didn't think so," Raider said pleasantly. "Good night, Bryce. Have a nice evening."

He stepped over the low fence and disappeared into the darkness, leaving a hurting and bewildered Bryce Wentworth alone in the night.

It was several more minutes before Wentworth shivered and began stumbling toward the safe, lighted security of his comfortable home.

Raider stood in the shadows watching. He doubted that the nasty, hurtful little barber would ever again feel quite so secure or so comfortable in that house.

CHAPTER NINETEEN

"And you don't have any idea who shot him?" Raider asked.

Doc shook his head. "It could have been almost anybody," he said. "Except Corey Finch and the few of his men who were behind me when it happened, of course. The reason would be obvious. Someone didn't want him to talk."

"That's the trouble with you, Weatherbee," Raider accused. "You're always lookin' for deep motives about these things. Could be it's as simple as some sonuvabitch being pissed at all the robberies an' cutting down on one of the bastards that's done them."

"Unlikely," Doc said, refusing to concede anything further than that in Raider's suggestion. "Most unlikely."

They were in Doc's hotel room, the door locked and the window covered. There had been a note, unsigned, in Raider's key box when he returned to the hotel. The desk man had said he had no idea who might have put it there, which was a good enough indication that the note had been sent by Weatherbee. It had contained only two words: Meet me.

Doc had told Raider about the events of his evening. Raider had said nothing to his partner, though, about Janie or Bryce Wentworth.

"No," Doc said, "I still believe it was someone who wanted to keep the man from talking. After all, he had already given himself up. If he was willing to do that, it was probable that he would have been willing to turn state's evidence against the rest of the gang to reduce his sentence."

"D'you think one of Finch's own people did it? That maybe they could've been in on the robberies? You know— inside information an' all that bullshit."

Doc shrugged. "There's no way to tell. The shot came from the shadows. It could have been anyone, in all the confusion." He sighed. "Not that any of it has to do with the reason we're here, regardless of what Corey Finch and his people may think. Tell me again about that business on the other side of the pass."

"I told you once already."

"So tell me again. Humor me."

Raider did so, abbreviating the telling this time. When he was done he said, "All right, smart-ass. What do you know now that you didn't before."

"Not a thing," Doc admitted. He pulled a cigar from his pocket, nipped off the end, and lighted it, knowing the smoke would bother Raider. Sometimes Doc wondered whether Raider knew just how much of what Doc Weatherbee did was performed for the purpose of deliberately aggravating the taller, less refined operative. "You say some more Chinese died?"

Raider nodded.

"And that you found no clues at all at the site?"

"Shit, Doc, what's a clue? There's drill holes in the rock there. I expect you could call them clues if you want. But I didn't find anything that would point to who drilled 'em. So by my sights, I guess I'd have to say I didn't find none."

"The drill holes certainly indicate that the sabotage is being well thought out," Doc mused. "Someone would have gone to considerable trouble—and time—to prepare the charges."

"That's what the crew boss said. A couple nights, prob'ly."

"No one heard or saw anything?"

"They heard the son of a bitch blow up. But nobody seen who done it. An' they hadn't heard anything of the drilling before that."

"So we really aren't any closer now than we were."

"I don' know. If I can find one of those boys I heard talking about the dead Chinese, could be I can learn where the rumor got to town. I mean, I can't see the idea of any honest traveler wantin' to cross that pass at night. So there's a good chance these boys heard it from one of the fellas as was in on the blasting."

"It's worth a try," Doc agreed.

"How 'bout you, then? You making any progress?"

"No."

"You figure to try something else, then?"

"Let me give it another day or two. Something might turn up yet."

Raider shrugged.

"Is there anything wrong with that?" Doc asked belligerently.

"Hell, no," Raider said. "It's ol' Rutherford Welles' money you're spending here, not mine. Me, I don't give a shit if you work on it till spring."

"Thanks for your confidence in me," Doc said. He sounded bitter and turned his head away.

"You got something in your craw, Doc. What is it?"

"It's . . . I don't know." Weatherbee threw his hands up in disgust. He shook his head. "I don't know. Really."

But he did know. He didn't want to admit it, but he knew full well what was bothering him: it was the fact of having to spy on a man, a family, that he truly liked.

"If you say so." Raider stood and helped himself to a nip from the flask Doc kept on his bedside table, then turned toward the door. "You know where to find me if you got anything to say."

"Uh huh."

Raider unlocked the door and let himself out into the hallway.

He cursed himself as soon as he had taken the first step out of the room, because he had forgotten this time to make sure the hall was clear before he showed himself at Doc's room.

He looked quickly in both directions.

There was a man at the front end of the hall, but the old fellow's attention was elsewhere. Besides, he looked like a drunk, weaving back and forth the way he was, blinking and staring at something Raider could not see.

Whoever the man was, Raider thought, he was no threat. He certainly wasn't paying attention to what was happening behind him.

Raider turned and went to his own room.

CHAPTER TWENTY

The miners Raider wanted to see did not eat breakfast in the same café the next morning, and he had no idea who they were or how to find them except through dumb luck. He wasn't willing to spend his day waiting for Lady Luck to come to him, so he saddled the roan and got an early start out of Tincup.

All around the town the rugged, sere mountainsides showed thin streams of smoke from morning fires at the mines that surrounded the town. The smoke helped him spot tunnel openings and shanties even at heights well above timberline, places where there would be wind and biting cold even in the summer months and which must have been virtually uninhabitable during the winter.

Yet the tenacity of the miners brought them to these high, isolated outposts and kept them burrowing deeper and deeper into the rock as long as there was color to be pulled out and turned into gold.

Raider doubted that he would ever be able to understand men whose lives were spent like moles. But he could not question their determination and their industry, even if he knew he would not have been able to join them under the best—or the worst—of circumstances.

This morning he was not interested in the mines, though. This morning he wanted to try again for some—for any— clue that would point him toward the men who were trying to block the construction of the Arkansas Valley, Tincup, and Pacific Railroad.

He pushed the roan hard to the top of Tincup Pass and stopped there to allow the horse a rest, once again awed by the spectacle of nature that surrounded him on all sides. The sensation was that of standing on top of the world.

When the horse was rested he moved it on again, slower this time.

He reached the end of the roadbed, but today there were no Chinese laboring to extend it.

Raider wondered about that for a moment. Then he realized that Crider would have had to pull the whole crew downslope to begin work on the trestle that was now necessary to span the gap broken open by the blast two nights ago.

He sat on the roan and looked over his shoulder, to the towering mountains still to be conquered by the patient Chinese.

The bed had not even come close to reaching timberline yet. When they did, Raider figured, the work would be even harder. Because then they would surely have to begin hauling lumber up the mountain to construct snowsheds to protect the rails and the trains from the slides that were sure to come each winter. The mere thought of keeping a railroad in operation here through the snow months should have been enough to daunt anyone. Not for the first time, Raider wondered if Rutherford Welles was out of his asinine mind.

He rode on, following the prepared bed with its easy

slope. Any gradient shallow enough for a steam engine to climb had to be as good as flat for a man on horseback.

By the time he had traveled a mile, Raider could hear the *chunk-chunk-thunk* of ax heads biting into green timber as workmen felled trees for the construction of the trestle or perhaps to make the thousands of ties that would be needed before the rails arrived.

The sounds came from above the roadbed, which was only logical. As long as there was suitable timber available above where it was needed, it was only sensible to cut it there and let the power of gravity help haul it down.

Raider reined the roan to a stop and reached for his canteen. As cold as the nights were becoming, the daytime sun was fiercely hot at this altitude. He could feel trickles of sweat starting under his arms.

His motion was interrupted by a sudden cessation of the sounds from above. The timber cutters had stopped their work. All of them.

Raider looked up the steep mountainside toward where the ax men had been working, but he could see nothing.

He damn sure could hear something, though.

The new silence was disrupted by a string of gunshots, one bellow of exploding powder followed quickly by a volley that must have come from half a dozen guns or more.

The roan's ears twitched, and the horse began to curvet and prance nervously. Raider reined it down harshly and tried to distinguish among the sounds.

Rifles, not revolvers. He was almost certain of that. Five of them, possibly. He could not be sure of that without knowing who the men were and how rapidly each of them could throw a lever.

The rolling thunder of the gunfire lasted perhaps fifteen seconds and then quit.

The sound of the shots was as quickly followed by the sounds of men screaming. Men with high-pitched voices shouting in a foreign tongue.

Raider wondered how many more Chinese had died this day.

His first inclination was to wheel the roan and charge up the slope toward the source of the gunfire.

But, damn it, there was no way he could get a horse up there. Not in a hurry. Possibly not if he had the rest of the day to accomplish it.

The roadbed where he now sat was nearly level, but above and below it the mountainside was steep and the footing was treacherous, with loose rock and thin layers of gravelly soil.

Far above him Raider could see a group of Chinese run into view, running as fast as they could from a thick stand of dark timber high up and to Raider's right.

One of the men fell as Raider watched. The unfortunate Chinese tumbled down the mountainside and landed face first on a jut of bare rock. Even from a distance of more than a hundred yards, Raider could see a red mass where the man's face should have been as the Chinese climbed screaming to his feet and began to stumble blindly about.

"Shit," Raider mumbled.

He pulled his Winchester from the scabbard under his right leg and turned the roan around.

There was no point in getting into too much of a hurry. Not now. He knew that. He wasn't able to charge the gunmen who had fired on the unsuspecting Chinese workers. Instead he would have to try to work behind and hopefully above them.

The odds were that the gunmen had used horses to reach the point of their ambush.

And their horses would be as restricted in these mountains as was Raider's roan.

Raider paused for a moment to think it over. Then, smiling, he spurred the roan horse and put it into a hard run back the way he had come.

CHAPTER TWENTY-ONE

Raider lay in a nest of gray, lichen-spotted rock. The roan was down below, tied inside a dense thicket. He couldn't see the horse from where he lay. The summit of Tincup Pass was seventy-five or eighty yards north of where he waited. He couldn't see the east side of the path from where he was, but he could hear any horses moving on the slick rock there.

And now he could hear a number of horses approaching.

There was the sound of a steel shoe sliding on the rock and then the distinctive clatter as a ridden horse fought to regain its balance.

A man's voice cursed loudly, and several others joined in with laughter.

Raider earred the hammer of his Winchester back to full cock and continued to wait.

The crown of a brown hat bobbed briefly into view and was withdrawn again, then reappeared, more fully this time as the horse the man was riding moved slowly up the slope.

Raider could see the crown of the hat, then its brim, finally the face and shoulders of the lead rider. Raider was sure he had not seen the man before, at least not wearing those clothes. His facial features were largely obscured by the brim of the hat and by a thick growth of dark beard.

The rider stopped his horse at the top of the pass—letting the animal rest there as Raider had anticipated—while behind him another rider came into view and then the next.

There were four in all. Raider expected a fifth man, but no more appeared and none of the riders he could see was looking back as if they might be expecting someone else to join them.

Looks like the whole load, Raider told himself.

He rested the forearm of the rifle on a rock and mentally ran through the swift sequence of events that would have to take place if he wanted all of them. The squeeze of the trigger, the flip of his wrist to chamber another shell, swing the sights onto the second man, squeeze, lever, sight, squeeze, lever, sight—a running shot it would be by then— and squeeze.

He could take each of them, one by one, before they had a chance to get out of view.

He *knew* that he could.

"Bitch," he mumbled under his breath.

The problem was that he did not *know* that this was the same crowd that had shot up the Chinese timber-cutting crew.

They almost had to be the same men. *Almost* had to be. The problem was the vast difference between "almost" and "certainly."

Raider cussed and grumbled a little more. But, damn it, he had no real choice about it.

He had to know that these were the *right* son of bitches before he pulled the trigger.

Damn it.

He came to his knees, exposing himself from the waist up, his rifle held at the ready but not aimed, because any sensible soul will react against the sight of some stranger aiming at him with a high-powered rifle. No, damn it, he was going to have to do this one by the book.

The men were talking among themselves. They didn't see him. One was drinking from a canteen. Another dismounted and began to fiddle with his horse's cinch.

Raider cursed himself for a damn fool and twelve kinds of idiot. Then he stood, his Winchester held at high port.

"You there!" he shouted. "Stay where you are. Pink—"

The man standing on the ground palmed his revolver with startling quickness and loosed a shot at Raider before Rade had a chance to finish his silly warning.

The gunman's slug whistled harmlessly wide. The distance was impossibly long for a quick pistol shot.

The distance was not, however, particularly long for a Winchester.

Raider shouldered his rifle and put a bullet into the man's chest.

You sure tol' me you was the boys I'm after, Raider thought as his muscles responded to his need without conscious direction and his wrist snapped down and then up again on the lever.

Too much time, though. Too much time, he was thinking.

Already they were scattering.

One down on the ground.

One hauling a Kennedy repeater from his scabbard.

One having a helluva fight with a horse that had gone crazy at the sound of the gunfire.

One running like hell down the trail.

Raider shifted the muzzle of the Winchester toward the one gunman who had had the presence of mind to go for his own long gun and squeezed off the shot. It took the man in the belly and dumped him off his horse.

Rade worked the lever again with practiced speed and

swiveled to his left, tracking the gunman who was high-tailing it down the road.

He fired. And missed.

"Bitch," Raider said as again he worked the lever.

Too much time had gone by. That one was getting away for sure.

At least that one was not interested in shooting back. He just wanted the hell out of there.

But why was the last man not shooting?

Raider brought the sights of the Winchester back toward that remaining man in time to see him lose his fight with the panicked horse.

The animal's steel shoes slipped on the cold rock. The horse tried to regain its balance, but the rider was yanking on its bit and trying to kick it into a run before it had its feet reset.

The horse fell. Man and beast alike tumbled in a hard, flat fall directly onto rock.

The man screamed and fell away from his saddle as the horse scrambled upright and raced downhill without its rider.

Raider tried to return his attention downhill long enough to get another shot off at the gunman who was racing away, but someone shot at him from the tangle of horses and bodies at the summit of the damned pass.

It was the man Raider had gut-shot. He was still alive and still trying.

Raider swung the barrel of the Winchester back again and pumped a shot into the gunman's head.

"Try shootin' at me *again*, you son of a bitch," Raider muttered as he worked the lever.

The horseman was out of effective range already.

No one else seemed to be shooting.

Raider stepped out from behind the protection of the rocks and walked carefully toward the men and horses who remained.

The two horses were standing nearby, although they were

nervous from the smell of fresh blood.

Two of the men were dead, the first Raider had shot and the last.

The man whose horse had fallen was lying on the bare rock with his right leg twisted into an unnatural shape. He must have broken it when his horse went down with him. He didn't seem remotely interested in shooting at anyone.

"Throw that belly gun away, man," Raider said as he approached.

"Mister, are you—"

"What I'm gonna do," Raider said, "is shoot you square in the head if you don't do ex*act*ly what I say an' throw that belly gun to where you can't reach it."

The man was already pale with shock and pain. Now he became even paler. He pulled a Colt revolver out of his holster and tossed it aside.

The gun came down hammer first on stone and discharged, scaring the loose horses and making them bolt several yards away before they calmed.

Raider shook his head. Obviously the son of a bitch did not know any better than to carry a live cartridge under the hammer of a single-action revolver. It was one of the ways damn fools could hurt themselves or, worse, other folks.

"Sorry," the man apologized.

"Looks to me like you can reach your buddy's gun too," Raider said. "Take it out and pitch it too."

The man did. This time the gun did not discharge by accident. Either he had gotten lucky, or the other man had been more sensible about how he carried his weapons.

"You gonna help me?" the used-to-be gunman asked.

"Likely. Who are you?" Raider laid his Winchester out of reach and knelt beside the injured man.

"Hogan. Joshua Hogan. You?"

Raider introduced himself.

"You one of them Pinkertons?"

Raider nodded.

The fellow reached down toward his leg and grimaced. "I expect you know what my problem is."

"I expect that I do, Joshua. Let's see how bad."

Raider cut Hogan's jeans open down the right leg. A pale, blood-smeared stub of bone stuck out through a tear in the skin. "I've seen better," Raider said.

"Oh, Jesus, sweet Jesus," Hogan moaned. "Don't let them take my leg."

Raider was not sure if at the moment Hogan was talking to him or to Jesus. Not that it particularly mattered. "Joshua, old fellow, our problem now is to get you down to where you can get some help. It's gonna hurt like hell."

Hogan began to blubber and bawl. "I can't stand pain, man. Never could. Even when I was a kid I couldn't stand no pain. You can't put me up on a horse, mister. You just can't. You gotta bring a wagon up to me. You *got* to."

Raider dropped into a sitting position beside Joshua Hogan and mulled it over.

He damn sure did not owe Hogan any great amount of consideration. Hogan would cheerfully have put a bullet into Raider's gut if he had had the chance.

On the other hand, he would not wish a horseback ride with a leg like that on anyone, no matter what kind of prick the man was.

And, hell, he was going to have to come back up with a wagon anyway so the two dead men could be hauled down.

It would have been pointlessly cruel to make Hogan ride while the dead rode in relative comfort.

"All right," Raider said, "but to make damn sure you don't think you're going anywhere without me, I'm gonna cuff you and lead those horses down with me while I fetch the wagon back."

"Thank you," Hogan said in the midst of a moan. He was still holding the shattered leg and crying.

Raider stood and retrieved his Winchester, then checked the two bodies for hidden weapons. There were none. He gathered the loose horses and walked back close to Hogan.

"It'll likely be dark before I get back up here," he said. "I don't think I could miss you this close to the road, but sing out if I don't spot you right off. You hear?"

"Yes, sir. But please. Get me a doctor. I couldn't stand it to lose my leg. I just couldn't."

Raider nodded. "I'll be back quick as I can." He swung onto the nearer of the led horses. It would be quicker than walking with them down to where he had left the roan.

He left without telling Joshua Hogan goodbye.

CHAPTER TWENTY-TWO

Raider found a deputy sheriff and the wagon at the same place, since the only deputies in the county were employees of the Finch line.

"I don't know who might end up reimbursing you for the use of the wagon," Raider said. "Don't know that it's a proper expense for the Pinkerton Agency. Maybe the county will do it."

The deputy, a thick-shouldered man with work-hardened hands and the scar of an old whip cut on his left cheek, gave Raider a dirty look.

"Mr. Finch," the deputy said, "don't ask no repayment for civic duty. Anytime we got to take for the lawin' is out of his pocket too."

"Sorry," Raider said. He climbed onto the driving box beside the freighter.

"Right up top?" the deputy asked.

"Yeah. Can you get a wagon up there?"

"Huh. Can a goose shit? Hell yes, I can get a wagon up there. Down the other side too if I had to."

"Not with me riding, you couldn't."

"Shows what you know, don't it?" The man probably was not much as a lawman, but he could handle the lines of a driven team. After a very few minutes Raider had to admit that. The fellow's confidence might not have been misplaced; perhaps he really would have been able to get a wagon down the narrow, slick trail on the other side of the pass. Not that Raider still would have been willing to ride in the wagon with him while he proved the point, but at least it seemed possible.

They passed quickly around the east side of the clear, quiet lake and through the rough, rock-strewn ford to the other side.

A long climb and a few sets of switchbacks and they arrived at the summit of the pass. By that time dusk had come and gone, and the sky overhead was a black satin drape littered with pinpricks of starlight.

"'Bout here, huh?" the deputy asked. His name was Efrem Smith.

"Yes." Raider stood in the driving box and looked around. "Hogan?" he called loudly. "Josh Hogan?" There was no response. He turned back toward Smith. "I don't know why he isn't answering. I damn sure never thought he'd try to crawl away in the condition he was in."

Smith spit a stream of tobacco juice past the wheel of the wagon and said, "His friend coulda come back and got him."

"His friend should have had no idea there was anybody left alive up here to come back to," Raider said. "The one that got away was moving his ass along pretty good the last I saw of him, and there was a whole lot of shooting going on. I doubt he would have come back."

Smith shrugged. "Coulda."

"Yeah, well, we'll see. D'you have a lantern?"

"Carbide lamp. It'll do."

"Then let's go dig Mr. Hogan out of his hiding place. The bodies ought to be on the ground over there."

Smith lighted the small brass lamp and followed Raider in the direction indicated. Raider was already circling the sloping expanse of rock, trying to spot any blood trail that might have been left behind. "Bring the light over here so I can see better," he called.

"If you say so," Smith said. "But I thought you told me there was two bodies." His voice sounded cold.

"I did." Raider turned. Smith was standing over the dead gunmen.

"Aw, shit." Raider hurried over beside him. The two men Raider had shot were there all right. So was Joshua Hogan.

It was no wonder Smith was giving him a chilly stare of disapproval.

In addition to the broken leg, Joshua Hogan now had a gaping, bloody wound under his chin.

Someone had cut the man's throat. The slash had been ragged and deep. And messy. Hogan must have bled to death within moments.

"Aw, shit," Raider said again.

"You told me he was alive."

"He was when I left," Raider insisted.

Smith did not come right out and accuse Raider of lying, but the disbelief was plain in the set of his shoulders and the tone of his voice.

"Somebody didn't want Josh Hogan to talk," Raider said.

Smith said nothing. He only continued to stare accusingly at the tall Pinkerton operative beside him.

Raider knew what the man had to be thinking. And Raider had to agree to one extent: it would take a low son of a bitch to kneel beside a helpless man and talk to him and reassure him and then cut that hurt man's throat. That would take one low bastard indeed.

"Shit," Raider said again. "Let's get them back to town."

Smith grunted. Then bent and began to help Raider carry the three dead men to the wagon for a slow and very quiet trip back down to Tincup.

"Well, damn it, what'd you expect me to do?" Raider protested. "I couldn't leave the sonuvabitch laying there with a broke leg, and I had to tell them *some*thing about why I'd shot two men to death up there. So all right. So I never thought about it. I went an' told them I was a Pinkerton operative an' needed help. I just never *thought . . .*"

"That's you, all right," Doc agreed drily. "Good old Raider, the man who never thinks."

"It's done now, damn it. I apologized. Now let's drop it." Doc Weatherbee was thoroughly—and, Raider came close to admitting, *almost* with some measure of reason— pissed because Raider had let the cat out of the bag about both of them being Pinkerton men.

They were having a drink together in a corner of one of the quieter saloons. Openly this time. There seemed little point in trying to maintain the charade that they didn't know each other.

Weatherbee sighed and grudgingly said, "All right. We'll drop it. You're certainly right about one thing. The damage is already done. Now tell me again about what happened up there."

Raider did, adding when he was done, "The onliest reason I can figure for someone to cut Hogan's throat is that they didn't want him talking. Likely couldn't move him— or as likely he wouldn't *let* them move him, him being so scared o' pain and all—so they killed him ruther than let me talk to him again. Must of been something like that, because none of the bodies was robbed. So it wasn't that sort of killing. Wasn't some stranger coming along and mixing into the middle of things. Every one of the dead ones had some money in his jeans."

Doc leaned back and fingered his chin. "Odd," he said,

"how very much the same thing happened the other night when I was taking that highwayman out of Sada's place."

"I hadn't thought about that, Doc, but damned if you ain't right."

Weatherbee did a rare thing. He let an opportunity for insult pass without taking advantage of it and made no reference to Raider's comment about not thinking. Instead he said, "The parallel is clear enough. One of the highwaymen who has been robbing Corey Finch is taken into custody but is shot down before he can speak. Now you get your hands on one of the men who has been sabotaging the railroad, and he too is eliminated before he can tell us anything. I wonder..."

"You wonder if because they do the same thing they got to be the same people, right?"

"Exactly," Doc agreed.

"I dunno," Rade mused. "Most can recognize a good idea when they see it. Could be just that. I mean, I can't see what connection there could be between the two different things. The boys as been holding up the wagons, I *know* why they're doin' what they're doin'. They do it to steal the gold them wagons carry. But what would that have to do with spending all kinds of time and work to bust up a railroad. Shooting some Chinaman or blowing up a rock ledge won't put any money in a man's pockets."

"I know," Doc said. "I don't see any direct connection either, but I have to wonder if there is one."

Raider shook his head. "Don't see as there can be."

"We'll see," Weatherbee said.

"You getting anywhere?" Raider asked.

"No," Doc admitted. "I've been spending a lot of time going through Finch's records. As far as he is concerned I'm looking for any pattern to the robberies of his wagons. So of course I really am doing that too, or I wouldn't have anything to report to him about. There is no pattern that I can see, although somehow, rather mysteriously, the shipments taken are always of great value. On the other hand, the exceptionally large shipments, when there is extra manpower and additional guards provided, those are rarely if ever bothered. The one exception to that rule was a shipment when Finch tried to deceive the robbers into thinking the load was of slight value. That time he actually used fewer guards than usual for a very large shipment. That one was stolen."

"I don't give a shit about that," Raider said. "What about our problem here?"

"Yes, well, I was getting to that. While I have been going through Finch's records for the one stated purpose, I have also been examining his financial books."

"What the hell for? You think Rutherford Welles gives a crap if your pal Finch is rich or not?"

Weatherbee shook his head sadly. "Sometimes, Rade, I have to wonder if you wouldn't be better off to pick up a hammer and go join those Chinese coolies laying track for Mr. Welles."

"Whoever is behind the sabotage has been spending a great deal of money to hire men for that job. Hiring men and even buying supplies for the blasting. You said yourself that there is no apparent profit in the sabotage. Certainly there is no immediate profit in it.

"So I have been examining Finch's books for any unusual or unexpected outlays. Men hired who do not otherwise appear on the work schedules. Unusual or inflated hours. That sort of thing."

"Shit! He lets you get into his records like that?"

"Of course. The logic behind it is to look for any recurrence of personnel in connection with the robberies. Looking for an inside source of assistance, as it were."

"So what're you finding?"

"Nothing," Doc said flatly. "Not in connection with the sabotage nor, for that matter, relative to the robberies of Finch Freight and Transfer. Nothing."

"Yeah, well, you been assing around wasting your time in that office. At least I managed to stop three of the sons of bitches. Those three won't be bothering the railroad no more."

"You can't kill a snake by cutting off its rattles," Doc said. "I believe you introduced me to that expression yourself, Rade, and it's true. Neither of us is any closer to finding the man behind the sabotage today than we were when we first arrived."

"You never know 'bout that, Doc. You want to see what's at the bottom of a kettle, you take a big stick and stir it around some. See what floats to the top. What I figure we got to do is grab us a big stick and stir like hell."

CHAPTER TWENTY-THREE

Doc came slowly out of sleep. He sat, then got out of bed and padded barefoot to the window. It was nearly dawn. There was a hint of gray in the sky toward the east; the first pale light would not be far behind.

Something had disturbed him, but he had no idea what it might have been. There had been no knock on the door, he was sure of that. Any distinct sound would have brought him instantly awake.

He looked out the window but saw nothing. Shaking his head he returned to bed. He felt a mild urge to urinate. He really didn't have to go all that badly, but if he ignored it he probably wouldn't be able to go back to sleep again. And he was far from being the early riser that Raider was.

He got up again, giving in to the inevitable, and crossed the small hotel room to the door. The place was too cheap to provide chamber pots in the rooms; instead there were common facilities down at the end of the hall.

When he pulled the door open, all thoughts of having to go were wiped away.

There was a familiar—and very small—figure curled into a tight, softly weeping ball on the floor at the doorway to his room.

She wore loose, filthy black trousers and a tattered and equally filthy white linen jacket.

Kwan Mei-lin's eyes, dark and moist and almond-shaped, raised to his.

He could see by the light of a lamp left burning in the hallway that the entire right side of her delicate, pretty face was a mass of yellow and purple bruises.

"Mei-lin!" He knelt beside her, picked her up, and carried her into his room, kicking the door shut behind him with his heel.

The girl was trembling. Now that she had reached him her shoulders were convulsing with spasms of tears. She felt as light as a bird in his arms as he carried her to the bed and placed her gently onto it.

"Where are you hurt?" he asked.

She shook her head.

"Where?" he insisted.

"It is nothing," she said. "Only here." She touched the side of her face. "It is nothing."

"Don't be silly. It's terrible. Who did it?"

She shook her head stubbornly.

Doc decided to postpone the explanations until he could get her cleaned up and feeling better. He stripped the grimy clothing from her—he hardly felt any need to worry about modesty after the time they had spent together before—and saw for himself that she had told him the truth. There seemed to be no other wounds or bruises, only those on her face.

"I'll be right back," he said.

He left the room and hurried down the hall, taking a few seconds to empty his bladder and then appropriating one of the hotel's towels. He dipped the cloth into the basin of water provided, wrung it out, and took it back to the room.

Kwan Mei-lin smiled gratefully when he gently bathed her face and then the rest of her slim body with the damp towel. She was no longer crying and seemed to be in little actual pain. He was sure she had been through an ordeal of some difficulty, though, and he had no idea why.

Or how in the *world* she had found him in this hotel room.

"Tell me about it," he said, sitting on the bed next to her and taking her hand in his.

"I did not know where else to go," she whispered. "I am no one. I am nothing. Excuse me, please. But you were nice to me. So I came to you. I will belong to you, if you wish, although I am not worthy of you." She turned her eyes away from his.

"Don't talk like that, Mei-lin. Tell me what happened."

She hesitated. After a few moments she began to speak.

Doc Weatherbee sat and listened patiently, letting her tell it in her own way, in her own time. He had to sort through and rearrange the facts to get them into a logical order. By the time she was done talking the dawn had come.

The story she so haltingly told was really a simple one.

Yesterday afternoon, when the shooting of the timber-cutting crew was reported, the Chinese railroad laborers went on strike. That was not the word Kwan Mei-lin used for their refusal to go out from the camps again, and quite certainly not the term the coolies themselves would have used, but a strike was what it amounted to.

Frightened for their very lives, the Chinese had dropped their tools on the mountainsides wherever they happened to be and streamed back into their camps, where they huddled together in the safety—and the misery—of numbers.

Welles had still been down on the rail siding in his luxurious private car. When word of the work stoppage was brought to him, he had been in the sleeping chamber with Wanda. He had been furious at the interruption. Even more furious at the news.

A work train had been close, Mei-lin said, carrying material from the railhead to the labor camps. Welles had stopped the train and ordered the flatcars exchanged for a linkup with his private cars and had them all moved to end-of-track.

From there Welles and his retinue had taken a wagon up onto the mountain, where the Chinese were wailing and moaning in their camps. Five more Chinese had died under the guns of the saboteurs, and the remaining coolies were too scared to return to their jobs.

Welles tried to bully and beat the coolies back to work.

He threatened them with permanent exile from their homeland if they did not immediately do as he ordered.

The threats had only increased the fears of the workers, who had already been forced to think of the unthinkable possibility that they might never be allowed to return to China if they walked away from their jobs.

The blustering and threatening only strengthened their resolve to remain where they were until the demon foreigners quit killing them.

"I tried to tell him," Mei-lin said. "I heard what the men cried out. They were afraid. As I am afraid now. I tried to tell him there was something he could say to them that would make them listen, make them return to work. They are obligated to work. They want to work. But he was telling them the wrong things. There were other things he could have said that would have made them listen and work. I ran to him, thinking to tell him this.

"But he was angry. When I pulled at his sleeve to get him to hear me, he swung about. He . . . hit me. Here." She touched the side of her face.

"I fell to the ground. The men roared. He did not know, I think, that they roared approval. I am nothing to them. I am worse than nothing. I am a thing that once was a person but is no longer of the home, and therefore they wanted him to kick me. I think he believed they were saying something else.

"He began to shout at them. He called them sons of

female dogs. He said it in our language. It is one of the words he has learned." She repeated it for him in Chinese. Doc did not bother to remember it. He had no particular desire to learn how to call a man a son of a bitch in Chinese. "It is a *very* bad thing to say to one of our people," she said.

"The men became very angry then. I saw some of them reach for their hatchets. The master could see. I believe he was frightened of the men then. He pretended he was only angry with me. He grabbed me by the hair and dragged me from the camp, kicking me as he went." She gave Doc a small, wan smile. "The sight of it pleased the men and took their attention from the master.

"When we were away from the camp he threw me from him. He told me never to be seen near him again, that it was all my fault, that I had stopped all the good he had done at the camp. He kicked me again and told me to go."

Mei-lin's voice broke, and again she turned her eyes away. "I am nothing. I have no place to go when the master does not want me any more. I walked through the night, where the railroad will be and beyond. I could hear bears in the night, and I was very afraid. I came here to you. I beg your forgiveness, sir. I did not wish to break your sleep."

Doc shook his head in wonder. The trip from the camps to the town was a hard one on horseback. How it must have been for a terrified girl alone in the night was hard to imagine.

"How did you find me?" he asked.

"I asked. I saw an old man on the street. He knew of you. He told me where to come."

Doc shook his head again, both at her tenacity and her luck. He wondered how she had managed to find the right room as well as the right hotel—probably by asking the night clerk—and would have asked her, but he was interrupted by the light, searching touch of her small hand at his crotch.

"You don't have to—"

He was interrupted again. His response was understand-
able. There was probably no other he could have made.

She was lovely. And she was naked. She was more than
willing.

Her small hand brushed aside the cloth of the drawers
he slept in. She found and fondled him.

"Look, uh . . ." He gulped back an involuntary croak.
"You really don't have to do that."

She rolled onto her side and ran the tip of her tongue
lightly up and down his shaft.

"You really don't . . ."

She took his cock into her mouth. She had to stretch her
jaw wide to accommodate him, and he could see the pull
of bruised flesh.

Mei-lin winced at the pain it caused her but continued
sucking on him.

Doc felt like a horse's south end. She was trying to give
him pleasure at the expense of her own pain.

"No," he said firmly. "Not like that."

He pulled away from her and stood for a moment to
shuck out of his drawers.

When he returned to the bed he lay beside her, wrapping
the protective strength of his arms around her slight shoulders and holding her close.

Mei-lin's hands crept shyly between them, touching and
caressing him.

She tugged, encouraging him, and he moved over her.
She parted her thighs and invited him in, cupping his balls
with her hands and guiding him.

Doc lowered himself onto her. And into her.

Invitation turned to acceptance, and the hot, wet flesh
enclosed him.

Mei-lin's arms slipped around him, and she wrapped her
legs tight around his hips.

He plunged deep and deeper within her, and she held on
to him with a fierce, possessive strength.

Doc held still inside her, enjoying the heat of her body. Before he could move, she began to do it for him.

Her pelvis arched up against him and then withdrew, up again and then she withdrew. Slowly at first, then with gathering force and speed.

She seemed to know exactly the sensations she was giving him, varying her timing, the depth and the speed of the strokes, to match precisely his faintest desire.

Doc held himself still, allowing her to skewer herself on his shaft beneath him as her tiny body pulsed and then— as his responses quickened and surged—frantically bucked beneath him.

Only at the end did he contribute, and that was beyond the last fragments of his control.

When the rush of pleasure could be endured no more, he threw his head back and bared his teeth in a rictus of pleasure, and the hot fluids poured from his loins into hers.

He remained poised like that for a moment, stiff and shuddering, then collapsed onto her slim, battered body.

Mei-lin accepted his weight and wrapped her arms all the tighter around him.

He lay like that for a few moments, then gently withdrew from her dripping flesh and lay at her side.

Her eyes were closed, and her breathing was slow. She was exhausted. Drowsily she murmured something to him in Chinese, then drifted away into the far end of sleep.

Doc left the bed and began to dress quickly. He hoped she would be able to sleep most of the day. He also hoped she could read English, because he didn't want to wake her to tell her where he was going or that she could get food from the hotel restaurant and charge it to him. He was sure she had no money of her own, likely never had had in her whole, short lifetime.

He felt a deep sorrow for her as he stood over the sleeping girl.

He placed the note he had written beside the dark spill

of black hair on the pillow and quietly slipped out of the room, his thoughts already on the task that lay ahead and not on the Chinese girl who remained in the hotel room.

He would try to borrow a horse, he decided. The damned, miserable bay animal was still at Corey Finch's stables, but the beast was too undependable and much too slow for what needed to be done now.

With any luck, though, he could borrow a decent horse from Corey and get across the mountain pass.

Doc shook his head in frustration and looked at the sun rising in the east.

No matter how quickly he got there he was likely to be too late. But he had to try.

He hurried his steps toward the Finch headquarters, planning already what he would say to Welles when he got there.

CHAPTER TWENTY-FOUR

Raider stepped out of the hotel, adjusting the set of his black Stetson on his head and enjoying the warmth of a good meal filling his belly. He had things to do this morning, and the first of them would be to learn if anyone could identify any of the dead men.

The only name they knew was that of Joshua Hogan, and no one Raider had talked to so far admitted to knowing Josh Hogan. Identification of the other dead gunmen would probably be as unlikely, but he had to give it a try. With any luck at all they would provide the break he and Doc needed on this one.

*Some*one in Tincup had to have seen at least one of those men. And whoever any one of them had been with when they were alive could likely point a finger at the rest of the gang.

He stepped down off the sidewalk and headed toward the barbershop. The other barbershop, that is. Raider was not a trusting enough man to pay for the privilege of having Bryce Wentworth hold a razor to his throat.

Across the street Raider saw an old man. He thought he had seen the man before. It took him a moment to remember. Then he recalled. It was the same drunk who had been in the hotel hallway the night he snuck in to talk with Doc in Weatherbee's room. A harmless drunk, Raider realized.

But his attention was on the derelict at the moment the man's eyes widened and the drunk began to stare with horror toward something.

Toward something that was taking place *behind* Raider.

Instinctively, his responses conditioned by years of rugged self-preservation, Raider dropped into a crouch and spun.

A gunshot boomed. The slug snarled through the air immediately over Raider's head.

If he had not dropped when he turned, Raider would have been a dead man.

The butt of the Remington came into his hand, his thumb hooking the hammer back to full cock even before the tip of the barrel cleared leather, and the .44-.40 revolver centered on the chest of the man who had just tried to shoot Raider in the back.

The Remington belched a lance of yellow fire, and the recoil rocked the grip back into the web of Raider's hand.

The assailant staggered, a heavy lead slug in his breastbone.

He used both hands to recock his Colt and try to raise it.

Raider shot him again.

The second shot took the man on the bridge of the nose and snapped his head back, the Colt falling useless from his fingers.

Even after life had left him, automatic muscle responses straightened the man's legs, stopping his backward totter, and when he fell it was forward, face down into the gravel of the alley mouth where he had been waiting for his victim.

Raider looked around, Remington cocked and ready for another target, but there seemed to be no one else in on the ambush.

Across the street the old drunk had disappeared, probably in fear.

Others were pouring out of the low log buildings on the main business street. They were running forward now that the threat of gunfire was over.

Hot damn! Raider thought. It looked like they were getting somewhere.

He did not *like* being shot at. But, damn it, it was a good sign. If the railroad saboteurs were trying to cut him down in broad daylight, then he must be closer to them than he realized. He definitely took the ambush as a good sign, a sign of progress.

Raider grabbed the first man to reach the scene by the sleeve. "Get Efrem Smith," he ordered.

"But . . ." The man's protest died in his throat when he saw the cold glint in Raider's eyes. He gulped and bobbed his head, then turned quickly and ran off down the street.

Smith was already on his way toward the sound of the shots. Raider saw him coming unhurriedly through the gathering crowd.

"How 'bout it, Smith," Raider said. "Recognize this one? Better yet, let me tell you. You don't know the man. Never saw him before in your life, right? Not you and not any of that bunch of freight jockeys you hang out with."

Smith gave Raider a look of disgust and said, "As a matter of fact, I do know this one." He looked around at the men who had gathered. "Half the boys in town know Curly."

A number of the people in the ring that had formed around them nodded agreement.

"Anybody know Curly's last name?" Smith asked loudly. No one answered.

"Well, I never heard it neither. But his name was Curly, and he worked collection and protection along the row of cribs up there." Smith pointed in the general direction of the section where Tincup's cribs and whorehouses were located. "Who he hung out with were the scabbiest an' shittiest of the whores workin' the cribs. He was most always around. If any of the girls had trouble they couldn't handle, Curly would come give them a hand. And when they got an extra dollar, he'd take and hold it for them. No idea what kind of split he got, but he never had much money. So, smart-ass, what now?"

The wind was definitely out of Raider's sails. A thought occurred to him. He looked up the street, toward Bryce Wentworth's barbershop.

The prick was standing there at the door to his shop. He looked almighty pale, Raider thought.

"Excuse me a minute." He took one step toward the shop and Wentworth bolted inside. Raider began to run, the Remington still in his fist.

He kicked the door of the shop open, fully expecting to be greeted by an eruption of gunfire, but the shop was empty.

Raider ran into it and through to the back. There was no back room, but there was a back door. The door was standing open.

Rade paused at the side of the door and steeled himself, then burst through it with the Remington held at the ready.

There was no ambush this time either. Bryce Wentworth was running for his life. Raider could see the man's back receding in the distance.

Raider ran after him.

Wentworth hurdled a low fence and raced through someone's back yard with Raider seventy or eighty yards behind. He ducked under a spread of wet laundry hung on a clothesline and leaped over a confused housewife's basket.

The barber stumbled, and Raider gained a few feet on him, taking the fence in stride at full speed and charging on. He ducked under the clothesline, but a pair of wet, soapy-smelling lacy unmentionables went with him. He threw them aside, flinging them onto the ground and drawing a yelp of protest from the woman who had just washed them.

Wentworth ran on, slowing slightly now, his pace becoming labored as he left the edge of town and started uphill.

If the man had a gun on him, he was not thinking of it right now. He thoughts were obviously on flight, not fight. Raider pounded after him, steadily closing the distance between them.

Wentworth ran across the road that led up to Tincup Pass and reached a stand of timber. He disappeared into it.

Raider reached the trees and had to slow. He had lost sight of Wentworth. Now he was trying to follow by sound where he couldn't see.

Wentworth must have had sense enough to slow down too. For sure he was not crashing through the underbrush.

Raider stopped and listened.

Far ahead—much farther than he would have expected—he could hear the snap of a dry branch under someone's boot. He moved slowly toward it, his hands busy while he walked punching out the empty shells from his revolver and replacing them with fresh cartridges.

He reached the spot where he thought he had heard the sound. There was a patch of bare earth between two roots of a mature fir. The print of a boot heel showed there.

Raider listened again. He was rewarded by another sound. But it was even farther ahead this time. He began to trot, moving as swiftly as he dared without losing his hearing, trying to balance speed against his ability to follow.

He kept on, mostly walking, sometimes able to break into a jog, steadily climbing, for the better part of an hour.

Unless he was awfully damned mistaken—and he'd be awfully damned embarrassed—Wentworth was still ahead of him.

But where was the barber going?

Raider couldn't figure that. Surely the man must know he could not hope to escape the whole damn country on foot.

His house, his family, his money, and his business were all behind in town.

Rather far behind by now. Raider had no idea how far they had come, but Wentworth had been moving steadily up and steadily away. Tincup must be several miles distant by now.

Raider came to a clearing and started across it. The character of the country was changing again. The trees were thinner here, what there were of them smaller and stunted in their growth. The slope of the mountain was steeper, and there was a great deal of bare rock on the ground.

Raider had not seen or heard anything of Wentworth in probably five minutes. He continued on in the same direction the barber had been taking ever since they broke into the trees down below.

He stopped. Concentrated on listening, his every attention focused on his hearing. He thought...

There. Again. He had heard it. Possibly the dull thunk of a leather boot heel on stone.

But it came from his left *and from below him on the slope*.

Had Wentworth changed his course? Or was Raider hearing the footfall of some innocent miner working his claim? Raider had already seen several shacks and shaft openings along the way, always off to the sides as Wentworth chose his path to avoid the mines and the men who worked them.

Raider had long since begun to suspect that Wentworth knew very well where he was going. The route was familiar to him, and he must have used it before or he wouldn't be able so easily to avoid the many mines that dotted the mountainsides for miles in all directions from Tincup.

But was Wentworth near his destination now, had he made some final change of direction, or was that only some uninvolved miner that Raider heard?

If Raider lost Wentworth now, he might well be losing him for good.

Damn it, it was a chance, either way. Whether he continued straight on in the direction Wentworth had been moving all this time or angled down from here toward the source of that sound.

It was the lack of sound that made the decision for him.

There was no ring of a hammer on a drill, no scrape of a shovel blade into gravel, nothing more that might indicate the normal, workaday sounds of a miner going about his business. Raider turned downhill, toward the latest of the faint sounds he had heard.

He reached a depression in the earth. Downhill from where he was, the depression deepened and steepened into a steep-walled gully. Upslope from where he joined it, it petered out in an outcropping of bare rock and a jumble of huge boulders.

On the slope leading into the gully, Raider could see no footprints, but there were several places where the gravel had been recently disturbed, where the specks of earth that were mixed in with the gravel that passed for soil here were darker than the undisturbed and sunbaked gravel nearby. Near the bottom of the depression those disturbed places angled uphill toward the rocks.

Raider stopped and tried to figure it. Probably Wentworth had run here for some purpose. An ambush? Or did he have something else in mind.

Whatever it was, it looked like the barber was hiding somewhere in those rocks up above. The land beyond the gully was nearly barren. Raider was sure he was still close enough that he would have seen Wentworth if the man had continued on across here.

And the mountainside above the rocks was completely bare of anything except more rocks. Nothing that moved up there could escape detection. Raider was sure of that.

The only place Wentworth could possibly be was right up there at the start of the depression. Somewhere inside the tangled nest of cabin-sized boulders that lay at the base of the mountainside.

Raider wiped his palm on the leg of his jeans and took a fresh grip on the worn butt of the Remington.

Slowly, very quietly, he began to edge uphill toward Wentworth's hiding spot.

CHAPTER TWENTY-FIVE

There was no ambush. Only the entrance to a mine tunnel, obviously abandoned. Very little traffic had gone into or out of the mine for quite some time. Apparently it was one of the holes that had not paid off. How Wentworth would have gained knowledge or possession of the place, Raider had no idea. But he was guessing now that this was Wentworth's private little rathole, the place the man must have prepared for himself in the event of an emergency.

Well, Raider thought, the man damn sure had himself an emergency now. Although he almost certainly did not realize the extent of that emergency. Raider was positive Wentworth never would have led him here. The barber quite obviously believed he had gotten away and that Raider had been left somewhere below.

Raider slipped silently to the shaft entrance and leaned against the solid rock of the mountainside there. He could hear nothing from inside the shaft, which meant that it probably ran deep and Wentworth had gone toward the rear.

Raider thought about simply staying where he was, waiting the man out. Wentworth had to emerge sometime. Raider could easily stay where he was and let Wentworth come to him.

On the other hand, Raider was pissed. Wentworth had tried to have him killed. He was certain of that.

Besides, Raider was curious. Why would Wentworth have made his emergency plans involving a place so distant from Tincup and so difficult of access? There was no logical reason for it that came to mind, not when there would have been so many other, more available places and ways to stash money, weapons, or whatever it was that Wentworth hid or did in this remote hole in the ground.

The choices were simple enough. He could wait where he was and let Wentworth come to him. Or he could go dig the man out of the ground.

Raider kicked his boots off so he could move more quietly and entered the tunnel mouth.

A box of candles and another of matches lay on a rock shelf near the entrance. Raider ignored them. He didn't want to announce his presence inside the tunnel. Bryce Wentworth was welcome to the belief that he had gotten away from his pursuer. Instead Raider ducked his head—the tunnel had not been dug with comfort in mind—and guided his way along the wall with his left hand while he kept the Remington ready in his right.

In an active tunnel or one that had once been a producer, that would not have been a good idea. Side leads and stope openings could turn a single tunnel into an underground maze in the total darkness. But a prospect shaft quickly made and as quickly abandoned was apt to have a single drift into the mountain. And Tincup was not an old enough camp for this to be anything else.

Raider eased forward silently in his socks. By the time he had gone a hundred paces he could hear movement ahead of him.

The shaft curved slightly to the left, the arc enough that he could no longer see the tunnel opening showing sunlight behind him. That was to the good. If he couldn't see it, neither could anyone deeper inside the tunnel. Wentworth would not be able to see Raider silhouetted against the sunshine behind him.

The dark was complete now. Just for the hell of it, Raider tested the ages-old expression. He stood still for a moment and held his hand up in front of his face. Damned if the old saying wasn't correct. He really *couldn't* see his own hand there, even when he touched the bridge of his nose.

He blinked, trying to see even though he knew full well that he couldn't. The sensation was an uncomfortable one.

He moved forward again. The sounds of some kind of movement were clearer now.

The shaft continued to curve. Raider got an impression of light ahead. At first he was not sure if he could really see a reduction of the darkness or if he was straining so hard for sight that he was imagining it.

Gradually, though, the impression gained strength, became a pale glow, then true sight as he was able to distinguish shape and texture of rock and even hints of color as veins of mineral intruded on the basic gray of the stone.

Someone up there had a lamp or lantern lighted. There was too much light for it to come from just a candle.

Raider eased forward more slowly now, careful of his footing on the littered stone floor of the tunnel. He wanted to make no sound that would give away his presence here.

The light came from an open area at the end of the shaft. Whether the vaultlike room was a natural vug—an underground bubble or pocket within the rock—or was an excavated stope he could not tell.

Wentworth was there, bending over a packing case. Raider pressed himself flat against the side of the tunnel and surveyed the room.

The barber and whoremaster had set himself up for comfort here. There was a bed on one side of the room, a chair beside it. Spikes had been driven into the rock to hold an odd assortment of implements.

Raider could not begin to understand their purpose here. Wentworth had brought into his private place a collection of thin chains, some harnesslike contraptions of leather, and several different varieties of whips and batons.

Odd, Raider thought.

On the other side of the area, where Wentworth now was, were several crates and a small trunk. Wentworth took something from one of the crates and put it into an open saddlebag pouch. He moved to the trunk, opened it, and began to rummage through it, occasionally removing an item and transferring it too to the saddlebags.

This Raider found logical, at least. The man knew he had been exposed. He knew that Raider was aware of who was behind the back-shooting attempt. Wentworth was preparing to run for his life. Raider wondered idly if the man was preparing as well to abandon his family or if he intended later to send for his wife. It occurred to Raider that he had no idea whether the Wentworths had children.

No matter. Raider's curiosity had been satisfied. He stepped into the middle of the tunnel and moved cat-footed into the high-ceilinged room.

He found it a relief to be able to stand upright again, without having to duck his head. The unrelieved posture was beginning to cause an ache at the back of his neck, which did nothing for his humor.

Wentworth had his back turned, his attention in the trunk. He had no idea that he was no longer alone.

Raider looked around the room briefly.

And his blood turned cold.

Jesus!

He gaped in horror at the forward wall he had not been able to see from the tunnel.

This place was much more than a place of refuge for Bryce Wentworth.

It was also the playpen of a sick and twisted mind.

There, hanging from spikes driven deep into the rock, were two bodies.

Both had once been women.

Both hung limp and shrunken in death, manacles locked around cold wrists, the chains of the manacles draped over the solidly set spikes.

Both women—what once had been women—were naked.

One must have been dead for some time.

But the other Raider recognized.

Janie. It was the whore who had been called Janie.

She must have taken a very long time to die. Repeated slashes of a whip had cut her breasts to ragged tatters. Dark, dried blood smeared her belly and legs.

Raider did not look to see what else might have been done to her.

He did not want to see.

He raised his right arm, the Remington extended. His hand was shaking slightly. Coldly and very calmly, Raider regained control of himself. He did not want any tremor to interfere with his aim.

With deliberate care he earred back the hammer of the revolver to cock it.

The sound cut through the silence of the vault with startling clarity.

Wentworth's head snapped around. The man's eyes widened in shock and disbelief to see someone—to see *that* man in particular—standing in this most private of secret places.

The man went suddenly pale. He tried to turn, but his knees gave out. He sank to the floor, twisting as he did so, so that he ended up on his knees in front of Raider in a posture of supplication.

Wentworth's mouth worked, but no sound came out. A thin trickle of saliva drooled out of the corner of his mouth and down onto his chin.

His eyes made the pleas his voice could not express.

Raider did not really give a shit what the man wanted to explain, what he wanted to ask or to offer, whatever vilely gained thing he hoped to exchange for his life.

Raider truly did not give a shit what it might have been.

The muzzle of the Remington moved slowly downward as Raider took close and careful aim.

His finger squeezed ever so lightly, ever so carefully, until the big .44 roared.

The recoil felt good in Raider's hand. He did not mind at all the loud, buzzing ringing in his ears nor the dust that drifted down onto him from the rock ceiling as the concussion of the explosion filled the stone vault.

Wentworth shrieked and grasped his groin with both hands.

But there was nothing left there for him to hold onto, nothing he could any longer protect.

Raider had blown his cock and his balls away, the slug of the .44 smashing them into a red paste.

Wentworth was saying something now or trying to. Raider was not really sure if sound was coming from the man's throat or not. The ringing in his ears was too deafening. Nor did he particularly care.

He took a step forward and looked with a critical eye down toward the damage he had already done.

Patiently he examined the extend of Wentworth's injuries.

With a sense of disappointment Raider had to conclude that Bryce Wentworth would not die from that one gunshot. He was not bleeding enough.

That was a pity, Raider thought. A real pity. He truly hated to put the cocksucker out of his misery, but if Raider left him like this the shit might live. That Raider could not tolerate.

He cocked the Remington again and aimed coldly down the barrel, his eye meeting Wentworth's as he did so.

He looked deep into Wentworth's eyes.

And pulled the trigger again.

Raider picked up a lantern and turned back toward the tunnel.

CHAPTER TWENTY-SIX

Weatherbee spurred the tiring sorrel horse he had borrowed. The animal had been hard used and was in need of a rest, but Doc could not spare the time for that now. Men are more important than horses.

With every labor camp Doc passed, his sense of urgency increased.

Because every one of the camps was empty. He had yet to see a single Chinese laborer, and he should have passed hundreds of them.

The sorrel, its gait choppy from exhaustion and foamy sweat lathering its forequarters, galloped around a bend in the roadbed. Doc sat up straighter in the saddle and drew back on the reins, pulling the horse down to a lope.

He could see the end of the tracks now, Rutherford Welles' private car was parked there still.

But between Doc and the car was a solid phalanx of men. Chinese men. All of them jammed together in a mass of humanity.

Above their heads he could see the pikelike weaponry of the Chinese.

Many of the Chinese had cut aspen saplings to make their pikes. Some had lashed knives to the poles. Others had simply sharpened the tips into lethal spear ends. The Chinese who did not carry pikes had hatchets, knives, even rocks in their hands.

From their throats came a constant, low murmur that Doc found much more ominous than any screaming or ranting could possibly have been. These were men with a purpose. Their intense determination might not be easily turned aside.

Doc came up behind them. Very few black-haired heads turned to look at him. Their concentration was all on the private railroad car sitting at the uppermost extent of the narrow gauge tracks.

The horse shied away from the mob, but Doc pressed his heels to the animal's flanks and forced it to push forward among the men.

"Let me through. Move aside, men. Let me through."

He forced the sorrel to the front of the mob, his eyes swiftly searching through the Chinese for someone—any-one—who looked remotely like a leader of this mass.

"You," he said, pointing to a tall, dignified Chinese whose eyes were bright with intelligence. "Tell your men to wait here," Doc yelled. "They mustn't do this to themselves." Doc prayed that the man he had spoken to understood English. If he did not . . .

Ahead of the crowd the white foremen and crew bosses had gathered near the front of the rail car. There was no sign of Welles, nor of the steam engine that Doc would have expected to find there. The private car had been dropped and left.

The Chinese Doc had addressed angled his march toward the sorrel horse. His eyes were locked on Weatherbee's. "You come to save Mistuh Boss, yes?"

Doc felt an enormous welling of relief. The Chinese

spoke English. Doc shook his head. "I came to save all these men. No matter what happens to Welles, if you fight here today you are all doomed."

"Nothing left," the Chinese said. "It is all bad. Better we die like men than leave our ancestors."

"Think, man," Doc said. "If you die fighting these people, do you really believe these same people will send your bodies back to China for you?"

The Chinese blinked rapidly. This was apparently something they had not thought of.

"Let me talk to them," Doc went on quickly. "Just for a few minutes. I may be able to talk him into solving your problem. And his. Let me try. For your own people's sake, not his."

"Maybe," the Chinese said.

Doc spurred the sorrel again, breaking free of the mob. The Chinese had given him no assurances, probably was not able to give any even if he had wanted to. But it was better than nothing. Perhaps there was now one man in the mob who would shout for them to wait a moment before they poured over the waiting crew bosses-turned-guards.

He loped the sorrel ahead of the Chinese mob. As he came closer to the white men at the rail car he could see that they all carried shotguns—short-barreled, ugly double guns more than likely loaded with buckshot.

Doc turned in his saddle and looked back to the still advancing Chinese. There were hundreds of them, perhaps as many as two thousand.

The Chinese were armed with the most primitive of weapons, barely a step above clubs and rocks—and some of them were literally armed with sticks and rocks.

But what in *hell* these fools thought they could do with a few shotguns against two thousand infuriated peasants, Doc did not know.

There were eight white men standing at the front of the private car. Each of them had a shotgun. Each shotgun had two barrels. Each barrel contained, if they were loaded with 00 buckshot, nine lead balls of roughly .36 caliber. Each lead ball was quite capable of killing a man.

But, damn it, even if every lead pellet in each and every barrel killed one Chinese, how many more Chinese would be left to club the white men to death?

The calculation was too high to think out on the spur of the moment, but it would be extreme.

The shotguns would not be able to cut down more than one or two dozen Chinese under the most ideal conditions.

Surely the guards did not think they could halt a mob with that kind of firepower.

Doc recognized Sid Kent among the guards. He brought the weary sorrel to a halt beside Kent, dismounted, and handed the foreman his reins. "Talk to them," he said. "Give me a minute with Welles."

"But what can I say?"

"I don't care what you say, man. Just keep talking."

Doc left Kent and the other whites there and ran up onto the platform of the rail car.

The door was locked. Hell of a lot of good that would do against a mob two thousand strong. Doc did not waste time knocking. He kicked the door in.

Welles was in his pigsty of a bedroom. Wanda, her makeup smeared and a loose, drunken look in her eyes, was sprawled on a chair in a most unladylike posture. Welles was standing in front of a full-length mirror doing something with his necktie. Doc could not begin to imagine why, what might be in the man's thoughts at a moment like this to make him think about his *appearance*, for Pete's sake.

"What do you want?" Welles asked. He sounded quite unruffled.

"Why, I don't know, Welles. I thought I might come down here and keep your own men from killing you. Does that meet your approval, or would you rather I leave now?"

Welles looked at him for a moment, then asked, "Do you

really think you can do that, Weatherbee?"

"Actually," Doc said, *"you* are the one who will have to do it. But I believe it can be done."

"How?"

"You've been lying to these men all these years. Bullshit about how they won't be allowed to go back home, ever, if they don't do what you say every time you say it."

Welles shrugged. The statement of fact obviously did not bother him.

"You need to do several things, Welles. First, you have to pledge to each and every one of those men a passage home, at any time they want it, no strings and no questions and no horse manure about job completions."

"You can't be ser—"

"You have to pay them their wages," Doc went on. "Every penny of it. Today, if possible. Within the week, certainly."

"But—"

"And you have to absolutely guarantee them that if they riot today, their bodies will *not* be returned to their homes. Those three things, Welles. Two promises and one threat. I don't expect you to treat them like human beings. They probably wouldn't believe you anyway if you pretended you were going to. But you have to level with them about being able to go home again—and at *your* expense—and you have to pay them."

"My cash flow at the moment is—"

"Your cash flow at the moment is damned well unimportant, Welles. You can't expect to build a railroad without a payroll. For that matter, you can't expect to build a railroad if you're dead. Those men will go back to their camps if you make those promises, though, Welles. I'm convinced of that. They don't want to die. They certainly don't want to be exiled from their ancestral homes. Tell them they can go back to their camps and wait there, that no more work will be done on the railroad until their pay has been met. And tell them you will make it a written contract guaranteeing them return passage to China whenever they want it. It's either that, Welles, or you and a lot of other people are going to die here today."

Welles pursed his lips and thought it over. "You really believe they would do it?"

"The payroll is money you already owe them. That won't cost you a cent more than you already owe. The passage, well, call it a form of insurance. Do that and you get to keep your workers and your life. Refuse, and I think you will lose both. But you do what you want, Welles."

"I like that business about not shipping them home if they are killed today. An effective threat, that."

Doc looked at the huge would-be magnate and thought about Mei-lin. It would have been pleasant to kick the fool where it would do the most good. But that would not accomplish much.

"Well?" Doc demanded.

"Give me a moment to think this over."

"Time's up," Doc said. He could hear the Chinese reach the car and begin to surround it. Sid Kent was saying something to them. Kent sounded nervous. But then he had every right to.

Welles smiled. "It might work."

"Then go do it, you asshole. Before people start to die out there."

Welles' eyes narrowed. "I won't forget what you just called me, Weatherbee. I shall see that your employer learns of it as well."

Doc threw his head back and laughed. "That is one thing I can say for you, Rutherford. You are *consistently* an asshole."

Welles left the bedroom and went out onto the platform. The squeaky murmuring of the mob changed to a low roar when the huge Mister Boss appeared, then quieted as he began to speak.

Doc shook his head sadly and reached for a decanter of

brandy on a low table in the bedroom. He took a drink straight from the neck of the decanter, then handed it to Wanda. She looked like she needed it worse than Doc did.

CHAPTER TWENTY-SEVEN

Raider was waiting in the tiny lobby of the hotel when a weary Weatherbee finally returned. Doc wanted nothing so much as a long drink and a longer sleep, but Raider grabbed him by the elbow and steered him into a corner where they could not be overheard.

"You look like shit, Doc," was his opening statement.

"Nice of you to notice," Weatherbee said. "But was there something you wanted to talk to me about, or are we just going to flash compliments at each other? I want a drink, Rade. I want a nice, hot bath. I want to sleep until approximately Tuesday. I have *not* had a good day, Rade."

"You can have your bath later, damn it, an' sleep till Wednesday for all I care, but first I want to ask you something. There's somethin' been bothering me all day today."

Doc forced his fatigue aside. When Raider spoke with this kind of intensity it frequently meant he was onto something. "All right," Doc said.

"It's something that dead shooter said to me when he was layin' there with his leg broke. I didn't pay it much mind at the time, but it come back to me today."

"Yes?"

"Hogan asked was I one of 'them Pinkertons', Doc. Like he already knew there was a team of us working here. Like he already knew there was more than one of us here. And I hadn't identified myself to them. I started to, but they got to shooting at me before I could get it out."

"Odd," Doc said.

"Damn right it's odd, Doc. So what I got to ask you is who all you told about there being a pair of us."

"No one," Weatherbee said. "I am certain of that. I did, of course, identify my*self* as an operative. Although that only to the people at Finch Freight and Transfer. But I told no one about you."

"You're sure o' that?"

"Positive," Doc said with conviction.

"That's kinda what I figured," Raider admitted. "I mean, there's a lot o' ways I can fault you, Doc, but you ain't an idiot on the job. I just had to ask."

"It does make one curious, doesn't it? That fact, coupled with the killings of both the holdup man and your saboteur before either prisoner could be made to talk. It makes me suspect there may be a connection between the freight wagon robberies and the railroad sabotage. Although I still fail to see the reasoning for that. But who would have known? I've told no one. I sincerely doubt that you have mentioned it. And no one has seen us together."

"I been thinking about that all day too, Doc, whilst I was waiting for you to get back from wherever you tore ass off to."

"I'll tell you about that later. Have you come up with any thoughts about how we could have been spotted?"

"Just one, though it don't make much sense to me. When I come out of your room the other night, there was some old drunk wanderin' around in the hall. He looked harmless as shit or I woulda mentioned it to you. But he was there."

"An old drunk?" Doc recalled that during the night Mei-lin—he had quite forgotten about the girl until this moment—had gotten directions to his room from an "old man." That was how she had described him. An old man.

Doc had *assumed* she meant she had gotten directions to the hotel and would have had to ask at the desk to find his precise room. But he had not asked her. He had not thought it important at the time.

Mei-lin had seen an old man in or near the hotel—which was another thing Doc had not thought to ask: just where had this old man been when she saw him?—and Raider had seen an "old drunk" in the hallway.

The same man? Quite possibly.

There was one man in Tincup who could fit both of those descriptions. And he knew from the Finch office that Doc was a Pinkerton operative.

"Old George," Doc said aloud.

"Who?"

"There's an old man, the town drunk, I gather, who works part-time cleaning up in Finch's office at night. He's something of a charity case, actually. I've seen him there at the office and bumped into him around town. Come to think of it, I saw old George in the crowd the night that robber was gunned down beside me."

"What's he look like?" Raider asked.

Doc described the man.

"Sounds like it could be the same feller, Doc. Now that I think on it, he was across the street this morning when Wentworth's man tried to blast me."

Weatherbee's eyebrows went up. He made Raider tell him about the incident.

Raider did so, but briefly. "It don't have nothing to do with the case," he concluded. "You could say it was personal, between him and me. Matter of fact, it was the old fella's surprise at what was goin' on behind me that tipped me to something being wrong. Or that sonuvabitch woulda put a slug in my back for sure."

"So George was not part of that plot."

"Nope," Raider agreed. "Which don't make him innocent o' some other."

Doc nodded. "We need to have a talk with George." He smiled. "I have a suggestion."

Raider bent closer and listened. A few moments later he walked away from Weatherbee and headed down the hall toward his hotel room.

Doc Weatherbee went to the cushioned chairs that had been provided in the lobby for waiting guests. He picked up a two-week-old copy of the *Rocky Mountain News* and spent ten minutes perusing it.

When he laid the paper aside he didn't head for the drink and bath and bed he had been so interested in a few minutes earlier.

Instead he went out onto the street and turned toward the shadowy streets and narrow alleys of the crib and cathouse district.

Away from the bright lights of the businesses and the busy saloons.

He sauntered along, whistling and smoking a cigar.

CHAPTER TWENTY-EIGHT

"Okay, Doc." The familiar voice came to him out of the darkness, from somewhere to his rear.

Weatherbee stopped his stroll and wandered back the way he had just come.

Raider was standing there. He was not alone.

"Evening, George," Doc said pleasantly.

Poor old George, Corey Finch's charity-case drunk, tried to run. But Raider had a firm grip on the back of the man's collar. He wiggled and squirmed, but he did not go anywhere.

"He was followin'," Raider said. "Just like you figured. Slinkin' along like an alley cat with a fat mouse to ambush."

"I was just going...over to Sada's, I was," George protested. He managed to sound indignant and quite innocently wounded by the accusation. "Over to Sada's," he repeated. "She gives me a drink now an' again. That's where I was going."

171

Doc smiled at him benignly while Raider maintained his grip on the back of George's coat.

"Sada's place is over that way," Doc said. He pointed behind them. Although the truth was that he had not been paying any particular attention to the places he had passed on his walk. He had not the foggiest notion of where Sada's place was among the whorehouses and rickety cribs of the district.

"But I *was*," George wailed. "I was just lookin' for a free drink. You know how it is, mister. You could buy me a drink, though. You'd do that, wouldn't you?"

Raider chuckled and said, "I been noticing something about our friend here, Doc."

"What's that?"

"Lean down closer to him."

"Must I?"

"Just do it. Tell me what you smell."

Doc made a face, but he did what Raider suggested. He leaned forward. An aroma of stale whiskey surrounded old George like a fog. "Ugh."

"Uh huh," Raider said. "Stinks, don't he? Just like an old dipso is s'posed to."

Doc nodded.

"Now smell of his breath."

"What?"

"You heard me. Smell of his breath."

Doc scowled, but again he leaned forward.

George clamped his bewhiskered jaws shut and breathed noisily through his nose. Raider grinned and smashed the palm of his free hand into the middle of George's back. A gush of moist air was driven from the aging man's lungs.

"Well, I'll be damned," Doc said. He leaned closer. "Do that again." Raider did.

"Wintergreen?" Doc mused.

"I got me a cough," George whined. "The doc's been giving me some candies to suck on."

Doc laughed. "Tell me, George, when was the last time you *really* had a drink?"

George's narrow shoulders shivered once, then sagged in resignation. He was caught and he knew it. "Couple, three days ago. I don' know."

"I think we need to have a talk, George. A private sort of conversation."

"How much?" George asked suspiciously.

"What do you mean?"

"How much you gonna pay me for what you want to know? An' don't bullshit me. I know you Pinkerton boys can give little rewards here an' there. I know you can pay me some for what you want to tell you."

Before Doc could answer, Raider stiffened, straightening to his full height. He towered over the cowed little "drunk," lifting him by his collar and shaking him the way a man might try to shake some sense into a pup that had just crapped on the floor.

"I got just the reward for you," Rade snarled. "You tell us what we want to know and maybe—I ain't makin' no promises, but just *maybe*—I won't break more'n three or four o' your bones before we get done."

George's wrinkled face became pale. Courage in the face of physical confrontation quite obviously was not his long suit.

"You wouldn't hurt an old man, would you, son?"

Raider shook him again, the old fellow's feet literally leaving the ground as Raider rattled his brains. "You ain't my pap, you old son of a bitch, and I'll stomp your balls to jelly if that's what it takes to open you up. Best you think about that before you start getting smart-ass with me."

George looked like he was ready to cry.

Doc feigned a yawn and pulled his watch from a vest pocket. He snapped the cover open and angled it to the nearest light so he could read the time. "Tell you what, Rade. I've had a long day, and I'm hungry. Why don't I go back to the hotel and have my supper. When you and our, uh, friend here are through with your discussion, you can come tell me what he said. Don't be long, hear?"

Weatherbee turned and started back toward the business district.

Behind him George had already begun to wail loudly.

"Don't leave me alone with him, Weatherbee. My God, you can't *do* that. I'll tell you. I swear I will. Anything you want to know. I'll *tell* you." ·

Doc smiled to himself and walked on.

CHAPTER TWENTY-NINE

"I don't understand, Weatherbee. Why are we going to the Lucky 7 at this time of night?" Finch asked.

"We'll explain when we get there," Doc said.

Raider, Doc, Corey Finch, and the four Finch freighters who had been legally deputized by the county were ascending a narrow switchback trail, their horses moving slowly.

They passed timberline and broke into crisp, clear starlight. The moon was rising in the east. By the time they reached the mine there would be light enough for their purpose.

"But—"

"We didn't want to chance any leaks of information before we left town," Doc said shortly. He stood in his stirrups and tried to see the deputy who was leading the procession. The man was supposed to know the way to the Lucky 7 mine, which in itself had been enough to make Doc suspicious of him. The mines that shipped crudely processed ore by way of Finch Freight and Transfer delivered their gold to the Finch headquarters. According to the records Doc had gone through in Finch's office, the freight line virtually never picked up shipments at the mine sites.

"Ray Nard is one of the nicest men in Tincup," Finch was saying. "Surely you don't think—"

"Just be patient, Corey," Doc told him. "We'll explain everything after we get there."

The line of horsemen negotiated another switchback and approached a natural ledge on the mountainside above them. The sound of the horses's shod hoofs on the rock was loud. Too loud for comfort. Doc turned and looked back toward Raider, who was riding at the rear of the line. Rade had pulled his Winchester from its scabbard and was riding with the rifle across his pommel. Doc unbuttoned his coat and made sure his .38 Colt was free in the holster. Just in case.

There was movement on the ledge up ahead, a black form moving against the lesser blackness of the night sky.

Their approach had been heard.

"Down!" a voice thundered from the rear of the column. Raider had seen the motion too.

Horses stopped, and men began to shift uncertainly in their saddles. Doc and Raider were already off their horses, weapons at the ready.

A spear of light exploded from the ledge, aimed down the trail toward the line of men and horses.

The lead horse screamed in pain and shied violently to the right—away from the wall of the mountainside. Its feet lost their purchase on the rock, and the horse screamed again as it fell, taking its rider with it.

"Jesus!" Corey Finch groaned loudly.

The guard up above fired again. The gunshot was quickly followed by the high-pitched, zinging whine of a slug ricocheting off stone.

The remaining men were off their horses now, taking

what shelter they could among the loose rocks that littered the mountainside above the trail.

Finch's men were freighters, not gunfighters, but they were willing. They opened fire up the trail, shooting blindly in the darkness but laying down a withering hail of lead that would drive any defenders under cover.

Doc sensed Raider's presence at his elbow.

"C'mon," Rade muttered. He began to scramble up the slope, away from the trail.

Doc understood immediately. Finch and his deputies could hold the trail and keep the gunmen occupied. It would serve as a covering fire while Raider and Doc climbed above the mine where they could pour a much more effective form of fire down onto the defenders.

Doc climbed behind Raider, glad that he had only a revolver, easily carried in its holster, so he could climb with both hands free. Raider was burdened with a Winchester too, yet he was able to charge up the mountainside with the agility of one of the shaggy white goats that ranged here above timberline.

Raider climbed to a point about twenty yards higher than the defended ledge, then angled across the slope until he and Doc were above the Lucky 7.

There were half a dozen gunmen on the ledge, each of them burrowed into protective nests of rock that looked like they had been placed with deliberate forethought in anticipation of a possible siege.

The defensive positions were an absolute protection against anyone trying to come up the trail.

But they were open to the sky. And to anyone high on the mountainside.

"Ready?" Raider asked.

Doc cocked his Colt and nodded.

"Then let 'er buck." Rade earred back the hammer of his Winchester and squeezed off a round into one of the rock-walled defense points.

Doc fired as quickly, sending a bullet into another of the strongpoints.

There was a scream and the clatter of metal on stone as one of the defenders dropped his rifle.

Raider and Doc fired again and again, lead raining down onto the carefully prepared positions that now had become death traps for anyone who remained in them.

The gunmen of the Lucky 7 broke and ran. Or crawled. They fled toward the safety of a tunnel mouth that was black against the mountainside at the back of the ledge.

Raider stood, the barrel of his Winchester tracking the last of the running gunmen. The rifle bucked and spat fire, and the running man crumpled to the ground.

"What'd you count, Doc?" he asked.

"I saw three make it into the shaft."

Raider nodded. "That's my count too. Countin' the one that crawled in. Shoulda shot him, I guess."

"You're getting soft, Rade."

"Fuck you, Doc," Raider said pleasantly. He turned and shouted down to the Finch men on the trail. "We got 'em boxed, boys. Come up slow now."

Slowly Finch and his deputies moved away from the rocks and began to walk up the trail. There was not a horse left in sight. The animals had bolted or fallen. Doc had not had time to pay attention to which. Regardless, there was no longer a horse to be seen anywhere above timberline.

"Let's go, Doc."

Raider led the way down, angling across the slope until they came down onto the side of the ledge. The mine tunnel mouth was a gaping hole in the mountain. They had no idea how many men might be inside or how they were armed.

"Damn it, Weatherbee, *what* is going on here?" Finch demanded when he reached the ledge.

Doc pointed toward the Lucky 7. "In there, Corey. There are your robbers *and* the boys who've been sabotaging the railroad. The same crowd all along."

"That doesn't make sense," Finch insisted.

"It didn't to me either," Doc admitted, "until their inside man explained it to us. It seems that the boys of the Lucky 7 have a good thing going here. They've been getting inside information about your gold shipments. They could pick and choose the ones they wanted to take. You know all the shipments you've hauled for the Lucky 7?"

"Of course. Ray Nard is one of our best customers," Finch said.

"As he should be," Doc said. "Because the gold Nard has been shipping with you is gold he and his men already stole from you. They just repacked it in new containers and shipped it out on your wagons. I suppose I should have caught that, but I never thought to cross-check and see if there were any significant absences on the list of customers of yours who had lost gold. But the Lucky 7 is supposed to be one of the best producers in the district. Yet our man says there's no mine there at all. Just an isolated hole in the ground where the men could hide out and relax between jobs. Every dime's worth of ore Nard shipped was stolen from someone else."

"Son of a bitch," Finch said.

"Exactly," Doc agreed. "Matter of fact, Corey, I'm willing to bet that this Mr. Nard, who you say is so nice, isn't named Nard any more than I am. It just occurred to me that if you say 'Ray Nard' as one word you have the French word for fox. The son of a bitch has been thumbing his nose at everyone right along from the word go."

"You're sure of this, Weatherbee?"

"We have an informant who claims it. And I would think that the response we got when we rode up here should be enough to confirm it. We'll know more when we get inside."

"But how can you possibly hope to assault a mine shaft?" Finch asked.

Raider grinned and spat. "Easy as fartin' in a tub, Finch." He raised his Winchester and shot blindly into the mouth of the tunnel, not bothering to take aim.

The sound of the gunshot was followed quickly by a howl of pain from inside the shaft.

Raider raised his voice and yelled out to the men who were now trapped inside the mountain. "We got six guns out here, boys. All we got to do is start shooting, and you'll be carried out lookin' like chopped liver."

"Wait!" a frantic voice responded.

"You said this same gang was trying to stop the railroad?" Finch asked.

Doc nodded. "We never saw the connection at first either, but it makes sense. They had such a good thing going from robbing your freight wagons that they didn't want to allow a railroad to reach Tincup. Aside from the fact that a wagon is much easier to rob than a train, it's against federal law to rob a train. But not a freight wagon. My guess is that this Ray Nard, whoever he is, has had some trouble with the federal government before and doesn't want any more. So between robberies they've been concentrating on stopping the railroad."

"I'll be damned," Finch said.

"No, but Nard and his men likely will be."

"Well?" Raider shouted.

"We're coming out," a voice answered.

"Stand aside, boys," Raider cautioned. "They could be bullshitting. If they come out with guns in their hands, don't wait for them to shoot first. Have at 'em."

A figure appeared at the mouth of the tunnel, then another and another until there were eight. One of the men had to be carried out by the others.

"Toss your guns in a pile there," Raider ordered, "and keep your hands where we can see 'em. You already made us nervous, so it's your business if you want to die for it."

The gunmen did as they were told. Finch's deputies bunched them together under their guns.

"Ray isn't with them," Finch said.

"You sure about that?" Raider asked.

The freight line owner nodded.

Raider stepped closer to the mouth of the tunnel and held his Winchester at his hip.

Quickly, as fast as he could throw the lever and trip the trigger, he hammered a full magazine of slugs into the shaft.

There was one answering gunshot. And then silence.

One of the Finch men started toward the opening.

"Not yet," Raider said. He reloaded his rifle and again emptied it into the tunnel. "Now," he said.

Raider stood outside the tunnel, waiting. A deputy went in to take a look. When he came back out, the deputy was gagging, trying to choke back an urge to puke. He lost the battle and his supper.

"I don't think Mr. Nard is going to bother you again, Finch," Raider said.

CHAPTER THIRTY

It was nearly noon before Doc woke from a much needed, much appreciated sleep. He opened his eyes and turned his head to see Mei-lin sitting in the straight-backed hotel chair with her hands folded in her lap.

She smiled when she saw him stir and immediately left the chair and ran to kneel beside the bed.

He could not help noticing that she had had the foresight to remain unclothed while she waited for him to awaken.

He took her into his arms and enjoyed the soft flutter of her lips and her breath as she traced a path of kisses from his neck down across his chest and onto his belly.

He had been too tired last night to enjoy her attentions. He expected to make up for that now.

"You feel better now," she said, dipping her head to trail the soft, tickling ends of her sleek, brushed hair over his erection and across his balls.

"Considerably," he agreed.

"I am glad."

Giggling, Mei-lin moved her head down and up and down again, her flickering tongue making brief contact here, again there, and back once more.

Doc groaned and stroked the warm satin skin of her back and buttocks. He slipped his hand between her thighs as she knelt beside him on the bed and gently explored inside her. She was wet and very warm.

Mei-lin began to moan. She shifted position to make it easier for him, then took him lightly into her mouth.

Doc pulled her body—so small and slim, so seemingly fragile, yet so vibrant with energy and purpose—on top of him so that she lay with her belly pressed against his chest, the rounded planes of her inner thighs pressed against his ears.

He could feel the cool flow of her hair cover his balls while her mouth engulfed him hard and deep, as if she wanted to capture him there, to swallow and keep him deep inside her throat.

She moaned at his first touch, then began to writhe and wriggle as he teased her to a quick arousal.

Her head bobbed up and down furiously as she spitted herself over and over again on the male hardness of his shaft, but even so it was the Chinese girl who peaked first.

She stiffened and shuddered, crying out in a muffled gasp around the swollen flesh that filled her throat.

Mei-lin rested for a moment, then returned her concentration to his pleasure.

Doc lay back and let her give him this gift. He lay very still until the rising pressures reached flood proportions and spewed hot and fierce into her.

Mei-lin stayed with him through the last shuddering spurt, then withdrew slowly, her tongue and lips pulling at him wetly, until finally he plopped free and subsided limp onto the nest of curling hair at his crotch.

She laid her face on his belly, her nose nudging against

him so that he could feel the warmth of her breath against the cool moisture that clung to him.

After little more than a minute his interest returned, and he began to build again, straightening and becoming longer and stronger with every heartbeat.

"Again?" she asked. She sounded happy about the prospect.

"Again," he agreed.

He pulled her around so that she lay cuddled in his arms.

Mei-lin opened herself to him, and Doc rolled onto her. Her hand searched between their bodies to capture and caress him, and she guided him to her.

"Ahhhh!" The heat of her was intense, and she was tight around him as he entered her and pressed himself fully into her.

He began to stroke in and out, the initial urgency spent now so that he could take his time and savor each sense and each sensation as an individual happening.

The hotel room door burst open, and that tall, laughing son of a bitch Raider stormed in with a broad grin on his face.

"*This* time, y'old bastard, it's you with your short hairs hangin' out," Raider roared.

Doc snarled and tried to lunge at Raider, but his position was not exactly intended for the launch of an assault. His legs tangled with Mei-lin's as the girl squealed and tried to wiggle under the sheet.

"You son of a bitch," Doc snapped. He lunged again, but Raider was ready for him.

Worse, Raider was still laughing.

"How many times've you done this to me, Doc? How many? Maybe you'll think better of it next time."

Doc lowered his shoulder and drove it into Raider's gut, shoving him against the wall with a crash.

The breath was driven out of Raider's lungs, but still the big SOB would not quit laughing. He grabbed Doc's shoulders and spun him around, then planted a big boot on

Weatherbee's backside and propelled him face forward onto the bed.

Mei-lin squawled and covered her head with the sheet. Her rump and the dimpled curves at the base of her spine remained exposed to full view, though, and even Doc had to chuckle—a little—at the rather fetching lack of coverage.

"Nice," Raider said.

Before Doc could jump him again, Raider straddled the chair Mei-lin had been using earlier. He propped his forearms across the back of the chair and took on an expression of complete indifference, like he had dropped by for a perfectly ordinary chat.

Doc shook his head. The man was incorrigible. Doc pawed through his discarded clothing and found a cigar.

"I thought you'd want to know right away," Raider said with a straight face. "Which is why I come here as soon as I got back."

"Back?"

Raider nodded. "Couldn't sleep last night. I was too wound up, I reckon. So I got up early this morning and went over the pass to tell Welles he don't have to worry about sabotage anymore."

Doc's interest was aroused now. Business first. He sat up straighter and lighted his Old Virginia. "Well?"

"The Chinese have all gone back to their camps. They ain't working an' won't till they're paid, but at least they ain't running around with hatchets looking for heads to lop off."

Doc nodded. "Good." He had been afraid the uneasy truce would collapse. Frankly, had he been in the shoes of the coolies—in their positions, actually; most of them did not have shoes—he would have been reluctant to accept promises and pronouncements from a bastard like Rutherford Welles. And the Chinese would know the man much better than Doc or Raider ever would.

"Good as far as that goes," Raider said, "but I heard

something that Allan ain't gonna like."

"Oh?"

"Mr Welles' private car ain't at the up end of the tracks any more. Seems he ordered the engine to come up and carry him and his car down to the Denver and Rio Grande tracks."

"You don't think—"

"What he *said* was that he was goin' off to the bank to fetch back the payroll money. What I *think* is that the son of a bitch has took off. From what that Kent fella said, Welles has already spent as much as he calculated the whole line would take and he's about halfway to Tincup. Got the worst of the mountain an' the worst of the weather yet to come. So what I'm thinking is that he's gone off to the bank, all right, but what he wants to do is grab what he can, likely including any new loans he can make, and rabbit for a hidey-hole someplace."

"When is he supposed to be back?" Doc asked. He took a pull on his cigar, then reached over for a corner of the sheet to drape over his lap. He felt somewhat too exposed the way he had been.

"Tomorrow," Raider said.

"Then we'll know tomorrow evening."

Raider grinned. "Whatcha want to bet I know what our next assignment is gonna be?"

"Finding Mr. Welles and extracting the payment owed to the Pinkerton Agency?"

"You guessed it, old hoss. That's exactly what I believe."

Doc looked reflectively down toward the motionless, sheet-draped form of the pretty Chinese girl beside him on the bed.

"We might need some information on the man's personal habits and history," he mused. "Ideally from someone who has known him well for a long time."

"Aw, hell, Doc, we could—"

"Now wait a minute, Rade. Think about it. It would be

a great help to the Pinkerton Agency. And of course such valuable help should be, uh, compensated adequately."

"What you're sayin' is that she's broke and don't have no place to go, is that it?"

"That is not at all what I said, Rade. I said that *we* may need help."

Raider grinned. "I hear ya. Sneaky old fart."

"Go away, Raider. I'll meet you for lunch in half an hour." Doc glanced down and noticed the delightful curves that the sheet could not hide. "Make that forty-five minutes."

Raider laughed and stood. "See you in an hour," he said.

Doc went to the door and bolted it behind Raider, then propped the chair under the doorknob to make *certain* Rade would not be back again.

He stood over the bed for a moment, admiring the shape and the texture of the dusky flesh he could see peeking out beneath the edge of the sheet.

Then he reached down and pulled the covering away.

Mei-lin rolled onto her back. Her eyes were dark and wide.

Her smile and her arms were welcoming.

Doc sank down beside her.

The interruption had been only a momentary annoyance, he discovered. Eagerly ready once more, he moved over her.

Mei-lin opened herself to him and with a sign of joy engulfed him with her arms, her legs—and more.

J.D. HARDIN

"THE MOST EXCITING WESTERN WRITER SINCE LOUIS L'AMOUR"
—JAKE LOGAN